"What Do You Want, Priss?"

Cooper asked.

"You."

The single word echoed in the darkness, vibrated between them. Still, he made no move to touch her.

"Maybe I don't believe you. You were afraid before. Maybe you still are."

"No." It was a lie of love, Priss told herself. It wasn't his fault that she had fears. She never wanted the shadows in her life to touch him. Still, her word didn't so easily convince him.

"Prove it," he whispered. "Prove to me that this is what you want. Show me that you're not afraid...."

Dear Reader,

Welcome to the merry month of May, where things here at Silhouette Desire get pretty perky. Needless to say, I think May's lineup of sexy heroes and spunky heroines is just fabulous . . . beginning with our star hunk, *Man of the Month* Cooper Maitland, in Jennifer Greene's *Quicksand*. This is one man you won't want to let get away!

Next, we have the second in Joan Johnston's HAWK'S WAY series, *The Cowboy and the Princess*. Now, please don't worry if you didn't read Book One, all of the HAWK'S WAY stories stand alone as great romantic reads.

Then the ever-popular Mary Lynn Baxter returns with *Mike's Baby* and Cait London appears with *Maybe No, Maybe Yes*. Maybe *you* won't want to miss *either* of these books! And don't pass up *Devil or Angel* by Audra Adams—just which best describes the hero, well, *I'm* not telling. Next, Carla Cassidy makes her Silhouette Desire debut with *A Fleeting Moment*. You'll never forget this witty, wonderful love story.

Yes, May is merry and filled with mayhem, but more important, it's filled with romance . . . only from Silhouette Desire. So, enjoy!

All the best,

Lucia Macro
Senior Editor

JENNIFER GREENE
QUICKSAND

SILHOUETTE *Desire*®

Published by Silhouette Books New York

America's Publisher of Contemporary Romance

SILHOUETTE BOOKS
300 East 42nd St., New York, N.Y. 10017

QUICKSAND

Copyright © 1993 by Jennifer Greene

All rights reserved. Except for use in any review, the reproduction
or utilization of this work in whole or in part in any form by any
electronic, mechanical or other means, now known or hereafter
invented, including xerography, photocopying and recording, or in
any information storage or retrieval system, is forbidden without
the permission of the publisher, Silhouette Books, 300 E. 42nd St.,
New York, N.Y. 10017

ISBN: 0-373-05786-5

First Silhouette Books printing May 1993

All the characters in this book have no existence outside the
imagination of the author and have no relation whatsoever to
anyone bearing the same name or names. They are not even
distantly inspired by any individual known or unknown to the
author, and all incidents are pure invention.

® and ™:Trademarks used with authorization. Trademarks
indicated with ® are registered in the United States Patent and
Trademark Office, the Canada Trade Mark Office and in other
countries.

Printed in the U.S.A.

JENNIFER GREENE

lives near Lake Michigan with her husband and two children. Before writing full-time, she worked as a personnel manager, teacher and college counselor. Michigan State University honored her as an "outstanding woman graduate" for her work with women on campus.

Ms. Greene has written over thirty-five category romances, for which she has won many awards, including the Rita for Best Short Contemporary book from Romance Writers of America and "Best Series Author" from *Romantic Times*.

One

"I told Mom nothing happened. How come no one believes me?"

"I think that you strained your credibility—just a tad—when your mother found you in bed with the boy, sweetheart."

"Not *in* bed, Dad. *On* the bed. We were just talking. We had all our clothes on. There was no reason for Mom to get all hysterical. And I thought you'd be on my side."

"I *am* on your side."

"Then how come I'm being exiled for a whole summer to the middle of nowheresville?"

During the long drive from Georgia to Iowa, Cooper had already answered that question a dozen times in a dozen different ways. His fifteen-year-old daughter simply wasn't ready to listen. Still, Coop would have tried yet another time if he hadn't been momentarily distracted.

The last turn was as familiar as his own heartbeat. Finally they'd arrived.

There was no parking spot in front of the Bayville Post Office big enough to accommodate a Lincoln Town Car pulling a U-Haul. So he pulled into the long blank space in front of the fire hydrant and turned the key. June sunshine, hot and healing, beamed on his face when he stepped out of the car.

For a moment he didn't move, just took in everything with thirsty eyes. Bayville, thank God, hadn't changed. The rolling hills of rich black farmland surrounding the town were infinitely familiar. The air smelled clean, clear, fresh. The white-steepled church still dominated Main Street. Stevens Hardware was still in business. The storefronts looked the same, invoking a hundred winsome, lonesome memories of his growing up years—years when he couldn't wait to escape his farm boy country roots and this "nowheresville" town. Back then, he'd wanted money. Life in the fast lane. Achievements, possessions, excitement, success. And no one could have convinced Coop that the price for those goals just might be higher than a soul's ransom.

But that part of his life was a closed book now. His pulse thrummed with anticipation. There was no place on earth as peaceful or restful as Bayville, and that was all he wanted from life right now. Peace. Quiet. The time to be with his daughter, to get back in touch with the values that mattered. In thirty-seven years, Coop couldn't remember a single moment when he'd had the freedom to be bored, but that was about to change, too. If a man could build a million-dollar company from scratch, he sure as hell ought to be able to teach himself to be lazy.

A few yards away, a woman climbed the steps to the old brick post office. Cooper's gaze wandered past her, then riveted back. Initially he couldn't have said what caught his attention. She was just a woman. Sprite size. Her clothes were nondescript—a sleeveless yellow blouse tucked neatly into khaki slacks—and she was juggling an oversize patchwork purse and a big mailing box. Her hair was cut shorter than his, scandal short, as shaggy as a mop, and of some indecipherable streaky color between blond and red. None of that was familiar. His gaze meandered down her lithe, slim figure to the trim curve of her hips. His eyes narrowed.

He knew that fanny.

Back in high school, when his whole life was ruled by hormones, he'd made a study of female fannies. Naturally he was long past that kind of immature, sexist thinking now...but he *did* know that fanny. With her head turned, he couldn't catch a glimpse of her face, but something in the way she moved and walked snagged another familiar cord. Coop was sure he knew her. Probably from high school. Yet he couldn't immediately recall anyone who was that pixie-short—at least six inches shorter than the fifteen-year-old who slammed out of her side of the car.

"This is *it?* The *whole* town? Dad, this isn't fair! They probably don't even have cable around here. What am I supposed to do in this hick place for a whole summer?"

Shannon's voice had enough volume to communicate her distress the length of Main Street. Cooper promptly forgot the woman and whipped his attention back to his daughter. "Whether you believe it or not, I hope we're going to have fun."

"Fun? Come on, Dad. The only reason I'm here is that Mom *made* you take me. I heard what she said about not being able to handle me anymore."

Cooper briefly wished he could strangle his ex-wife, Denise, for making that comment in Shannon's hearing. His tone gentled. "Neither your mother nor her husband *made* me take you, kiddo. I *wanted* you with me. You don't have to stay beyond the summer if you don't want to, but you and I have had too little time together since the divorce. I'm serious about moving back here, and Bayville is part of your roots. You know how much you loved Gramps. If nothing else, this is a chance to show you how he lived, how I lived growing up, what that whole side of your family is about."

His daughter rolled her eyes. "Horse patooties. You just all want me away from Tim."

"That, too," Cooper admitted dryly.

"Nothing you can do will make me fall out of love with him. *Nothing*. I don't care what you say. I don't care what you do. You just don't understand about being in love. I . . . I . . ."

Shannon's head turned. Cooper followed the direction of her gaze. Across the street, a boy pushed open the door to the hardware store, leaned against the side of the building and flipped the lid on a soda. His sandy hair was short, clean-cut. He was wearing working jeans and a white T-shirt and his skin was tanned to a honey bronze. The boy had a set of biceps and shoulders that made Cooper suspect he came from good farm stock and had known his share of physical work.

Shannon also noticed those biceps and shoulders, but regrettably from a different perspective. Cooper watched his daughter straighten. She tossed back her hair—her long, blond, permed, spritzed and moussed hair that took her half an hour every morning to achieve that just-caught-in-a-fan look. Nubile, budding breasts jutted forward. A slim hand perched on her hip. Maybe, Cooper thought, he could just send her to a nunnery until she was forty or so.

"I have to go in the post office to pick up keys and some papers and set up mail..."

Shannon vaguely waved him on. So far she hadn't taken her eyes off the boy. "I'll stay here."

"It's hot. You'll bake in the sun, and it's going to take me a few minutes—"

Suddenly his daughter's tone turned judiciously helpful. "Someone has to stay with the car and trailer. What if a policeman comes by? I can at least explain why we're parked in front of the fire hydrant. Just go on, Dad. I'll be fine."

Cooper decided it was an expedient moment to make a parental concession. "When we get to Gramp's house, you can call Tim." When there was no response, he tried again. "Tim? You know, the boy you're madly in love with?"

"Hmm."

By the end of the summer, Cooper figured, his brown hair was likely to turn stark white. As he zipped up the steps to the post office, he specifically recalled the day Shannon was born, how much he'd wanted a daughter, the idealistic visions he'd had of spoiling and cuddling a sweet bundle of femininity. At no time had he imagined a five-foot-ten fifteen-year-old with a centerfold figure, a double dose of hormones and a looking-for-trouble temperament that, damnation, she'd inherited from him.

As Cooper swung open the heavy wooden door, he mentally corrected that thought. He wasn't looking for trouble anymore, any kind of trouble, and if there was a place on earth where he could turn his daughter around before she followed in his mistaken footsteps, it had to be here.

One glance inside the post office reaffirmed the accuracy of his decision to come home. The wooden plank floor, the smells of ink and glue, the squeak of the old-fashioned ceiling fan were all familiar. Things in Bayville were built to last. No one messed up their lives in a pressure cooker of eighty-hour workweeks. The life was slower paced; the old values endured and people made time for each other. Coop's mouth cracked in a grin when he recognized Joella behind the counter. She'd been an institution at the post office when he was a kid. Her hair was graying and wispy now, but she still wore small round lenses perched on the edge of her nose, still had a half-chewed pencil stuck behind her ear.

The pixie was in there, too—waiting in line to mail that monster-size box. Cooper quietly stepped behind her, prepared to be patient. If he remembered right, Joella never let a customer escape without a full quota of gossip.

An older man in bib overalls turned around; then it was the pixie's turn. As Cooper expected, Joella began the grilling. ''How's Matthew doing?''

''Matt's just fine,'' the pixie responded. ''Working at the hardware store for the summer. It's long hours, but he has his heart set on earning enough money to buy a car.''

"Hard work never hurt anyone. You've got a good boy there, Priss. Says a lot for how you've raised him. I know it hasn't been easy for you since David died. This package for your sister? In California now, is she?"

Cooper, half listening, gathered that the pixie was probably the mother of the boy he'd seen outside the hardware store. His interest wasn't fully aroused, though, until he caught the name "Priss."

Faster than heat lightning, a dozen memories slashed through his mind. Priscilla Wilson. Priss. The full of hell, full of fun, most unlikely minister's daughter. She'd been a year behind him in school, but they'd shared a few classes. She couldn't stand school—always forgot her homework, never had a pen—but if there was fun to be had, Priss was likely the instigator. He still remembered that she had an incredible laugh—exuberant and mischievous, full of life and joy, as infectious as a case of measles and the exasperating bane of every teacher she'd ever had.

He couldn't resist. "Priss Wilson?"

She turned her head. Joella looked up. Both recognized him at the same time. "Well, Cooper Maitland! I heard all about your coming back home, but I wasn't going to believe it until I saw the whites of your eyes! We were all so sorry about your dad."

Joella strode around the counter. Cooper heard her warm welcome, accepted her bony hug, even heard himself responding with appropriate comments, but he could hardly take his eyes off Priss.

The change in her startled him. She'd grown up, of course. The hopeless giggler had matured, which was hardly a surprise. But he remembered a girl with a wild mane of carroty-bright hair bouncing down her back, a flat boyish figure and a streak of freckles across her nose. Since she'd never been pretty, Cooper had no reason to suspect that she would turn out stunning.

But stunning she was. Her hair still had some copper, but the shade had softened to a sun-shot taffy, striking and distinctive. The severely short cut should have looked mannish, but not on her. Spiky bangs fringed her forehead and feathered around the delicate shell of her ears, showing off feminine fine bones and the sassy line of her jaw.

A few freckles still dotted the bridge of her nose. Not many. Her cheeks had the kiss of color, her skin the pure translucence of ivory. She'd always had huge brown eyes—quick and bright—but she wasn't an impulsive, innocent girl anymore and it showed. Her face was carved with character. She had a woman's eyes now, deep and dark, filled with a woman's secrets and 'a woman's sensuality.

Joella kept talking, chattering on about town news. Priss met Cooper's eyes for a brief second, sharing mutual humor that there was nothing either of them could do to stop Joella's gregarious onslaught. But her smile cooled and he saw her shoulders stiffen when she realized he was staring.

Cooper never meant to stare, but damned if he could make himself look away. His interest was purely objective, he told himself judiciously. Feeling curious about someone he once knew was only natural.

His gaze strayed—objectively—to her mouth. She had soft lips, small lips, the upper one shaped in a delicate M. Cooper couldn't remember the last time he'd noticed a woman's mouth; for two years he'd been living the life-style of a monk, but even a monk couldn't help but—objectively—notice that she was no longer boyishly flat. No centerfold voluptuousness. No extras. But she definitely filled out that yellow blouse with an alluringly snug set of curves.

Her eyes darted back to his, then away. That small, square chin tilted up, just a hair. She'd be lucky to reach a pip-squeak five foot three in heels, but she still managed to give off *watch it, buster, nobody messes with me* vibrations. Cooper mentally swore at himself for making her nervous . . . but darned if he could entirely hold back a grin. At six foot two, he towered over her by almost a foot. In the business world, his size alone had a way of intimidating people. He liked a woman—always had, always would—who could hold her own.

Years ago they'd never been close, but he'd always liked the irrepressible elf. Now though, there was strength and experience in her face—no toughness, just the gutsiness of a woman who'd come into her own. And those dark, sensual eyes were full of mystery. Once, Cooper had been addicted to challenges. No puzzle was any fun unless it was impossibly complex. And Priss Wilson had changed so much that he was—objectively—intrigued at the reason.

"Priss Neilson now," she informed him. Her voice was a husky alto that made him think of long nights and smoky sex, but the tone was as cool as a spring frost. "So you're here with your daughter?"

"Yes. At least for now—technically Shannon's only with me for the summer. When school starts in the fall, she's supposed to go back to Atlanta with her mother."

"Well, it looks like we'll be neighbors in the meantime. My son and I are in the white house with the blue shutters, just a stone's throw from your dad's place. If you need any help, just sing out."

"Thanks."

It was a neighborly offer, nothing more implied. And she offered a smile, but it disappeared so swiftly that Cooper clearly understood she was miffed at him for looking her over. No question, he thought dryly, that the sharp, hot tug of sexual voltage was all on his side.

As unexpected as it was, Coop liked that tug. He had always been comfortable with his own sexuality. It had been years since he'd felt that unpredictable ambush of hormones, that sizzle-sharp awareness of a woman...but truthfully, it was just as well that Priss didn't return the attraction. He'd come home to strip his life of complications, not to add any. The only challenge allowed on the horizon was his daughter, and Shannon needed all the one-on-one time he could give her. He wasn't against becoming involved with a woman—it had been five years since the divorce—but good grief. Not now.

Still, when Priss exited through the heavy door, he found himself staring after her.

"Isn't she adorable?"

Cooper jerked his head back to the postmistress. "Pardon?"

"Priss. Didn't she turn out something?"

"I...um...yes." Cooper thought that he should have known better than to look at anyone sideways in front of the town's worst gossip.

Joella had been holding his father's keys and a sheath of legal papers for his arrival. She handed him the bundle, then began the process of assigning him a P.O. box. "She's been alone five years now since Da-

vid was killed in a tractor accident. You knew David
Neilson from school, didn't you?''

"She was married to *that* Neilson? David?'' Cooper's brows shot up in surprise. He vaguely remembered the stocky, stodgy, dull-eyed farm boy. Priss had
been smart and sassy, vibrant, full of emotion and
laughter. For the life of him, he couldn't imagine how
or why she'd ever hooked up with David.

"She raised Matt by herself since. Teaches biology
in the high school—''

"She teaches? Priss? You're kidding.'' Another total impossibility. The Priss he remembered had hated
school with a vocal and violent passion.

"She does. Wonderful at it, too. Can't say there
isn't a soul in town who doesn't love her. We've all
tried to fix her up, but she just won't go out. Too busy,
she says. But she's just so darling that we all hate to see
her alone.'' Having imparted that wealth of information, Joella pushed the spectacles back on her nose.
There was an etiquette to gossip. First one sowed.
Then—when one's victim was distracted, and Cooper
was focusing speculatively on the door where Priss left
with a wonderfully distracted frown—one reaped. "Is
that Lincoln Town Car out there yours? Of course,
your father was always telling us how successful you
were, Coop. Do you *really* intend to settle back in
Bayville...?''

The minute Priss stepped out into the sunshine, the
air expelled from her lungs in a little whoosh.

After finishing her chores in town, she'd intended
to drop by the rectory to chitchat with her dad.
Thankfully her dad wasn't expecting her, because she
abruptly changed her mind. She sprinted across Main

Street, climbed into her white Saturn and headed straight home.

Halfway through town, she kicked off her sandals and drove barefoot. Once on the highway, she thumbed open the top two buttons of her blouse and let the wind caress her throat, run through her hair. Teachers were expected to maintain a certain image in Bayville. Priss didn't buck the system. There wasn't a soul who'd ever know she drove barefoot when she was alone, and besides, she was hot. Hot, rattled and edgy.

The baking June day was responsible for the temperature, and Priss got rattled over lots of things—Matt learning how to drive, Cleopatra having a litter of kittens, overdrawn bank accounts, the future, the past, dentist appointments...the list was endless. She tended to respond emotionally to things, with one notable exception. Men. Priss hadn't been rattled by a man—or allowed herself to become rattled—in years.

It was the way Cooper had looked her up and down. Thoroughly. As if she was a country he'd sure like to take over. As if he definitely appreciated the look of her engine. As if, damnation, he didn't mind her knowing that he was sexually interested.

Impatiently Priss flipped on the car radio and tuned to farm news. There was nothing more boring than farm news. A few minutes of listening to grain market prices was guaranteed to take the edgy flutter out of her pulse. Only it didn't seem to work. Like a sliver had been imbedded under her skin, her thoughts kept sneaking back to Cooper.

She'd been startled that he even remembered her—except, maybe, as the giggly, bouncy klutz she'd been in high school. They'd known each other, but only in the sense that everyone knew everyone in a small town. She remembered him giving her an occasional ride to school, sharing a couple of classes. She'd dated lots of boys, but never Coop. Even if they hadn't been polar opposites in personality, Cooper had been going with a girl all through high school—Lainie Roberts—and everyone knew they were sleeping together.

If Lainie did half the things with Coop that she'd claimed in the girls' locker room after fourth-hour gym...well, Priss had listened, just as bug-eyed and enthralled as everyone else. But Lainie had been positive that marriage was in the offing. Priss might have believed the sexual exploits, but she'd never believed the wedding-bell future. Containing Cooper Maitland in a small town like Bayville was like expecting a caged panther to be happy.

He'd always been driven. Restless, impatient, a high-voltage package of energy and ideas and ambition. That he'd turned into a mover and a shaker in Atlanta had never surprised Priss. Even as a kid, he'd set goals and then gone after them like a charging bull, full speed ahead and God help anything that was in his way. She'd always liked him. Why not? Excitement trailed in Cooper's wake. He'd been sinfully good-looking—thick brown hair, Paul Newman blue eyes, and a grin charged with sexual energy. More relevant, he'd always been kind to her.

Her heart was still bucking like an uneasy colt, and her palms were slippery damp on the steering wheel. Foolishness, she chided herself. When his shrewd blue eyes had swept over her figure, she'd just been...startled. He was damn near tall enough to reach the ozone layer, and the width of his shoulders hadn't shrunk. His face had lines now, his hair a few streaks of silver, but age hadn't diminished his particular brand of dynamite. The brash confidence of the boy was gone, but the vital, restless male energy was still there. Yet more potent now. More unignorable. In his eyes was the strength and experience of a man who'd known power, used it and liked it. His smile had more sexual wattage than a direct hit of lightning, and when he'd turned that smile on her, she'd felt a shock of vulnerability, a shivery sensation of feeling overpowered by something she couldn't control.

Priss glanced at her reflection in the rearview mirror. *Nobody was overpowering anybody. What on earth is the matter with you? Are you gonna be a goose and dwell on this all afternoon?*

Minutes later she turned into the gravel driveway and pulled up beneath the shade of the old, gray-barked hickory. Once she shut off the engine, the yard was silent, peaceful. And comfortingly familiar.

David had built her the white bungalow a few years after Matthew was born. Morning glories climbed the porch posts, blooming in a riot of color. Finches were having a field day under the feeder; sassy yellow dandelions were sprouting all through the grass. The tree swing, a relic from Matt's childhood, swayed from the arms of the giant oak in the backyard, propelled by a silky, sultry breeze.

Gradually her heartbeat climbed down. This was home. She felt safe here. She still missed David, missed his steadying presence even after all this time, but she'd had no nightmares for years now. David had always been understanding and patient when she had those bad dreams. Not Priss. She didn't believe in dwelling on problems.

A long time ago she'd discovered one of the universal truths unique to women. Through feast, famine, tornadoes or floods, dirty dishes that someone had to wash were still going to accumulate in the sink—and inevitably that "someone" was a woman. Life didn't stop for a crisis. Women coped. When something bad happened, you put it behind you, picked yourself up, squared your chin and went on. It was how Priss lived, what she believed, what she expected of herself. And through the years, she'd proven to herself—with or without David—that she could do a first-rate, grade-A job of coping.

Slowly Priss stepped out of the car and glanced at the sprawling frame farmhouse a hundred yards away. Her closest neighbor had been Cooper's father. When George Maitland died, the town had bubbled for days with the news that Cooper was coming home—not just to settle his father's affairs, but actually intending to move into the old family farmhouse.

When cats flew, Priss thought, and suddenly chuckled. After only a few minutes with Coop, it was obvious that he hadn't changed. Bayville would bore him witless in a week. She'd loved George, but he'd really let the place go in the past few years. It was going to take Cooper some time to get the old house in order and put the farm property up for sale, but after that—Priss had no doubt—he'd be out of here.

She'd help them all she could, she mused, and then shook her head impatiently. Grabbing her sandals and purse, she headed for the porch. How silly she was to let herself get all rattled over nothing. Cooper Maitland couldn't help being dynamite. It's just the way he was.

And if there was one thing on earth Priss was sure of, it was her own ability to cope. With dynamite or anything else.

Two

"Okay with you if I go to a movie tonight?"

Priss watched her son eat, a similar experience to watching water pour down a drain. Three glasses of milk, a mountainous baked potato and a triple serving of meat loaf—gone, in the blink of an eye. "Sure, as long as you're not out too late. Going with anyone special?"

"Jason got his license. His dad said he could use the car, so he's picking up Suze and Frawley, and I told Shannon she could go with us if she wanted. No big deal. We'll probably stop for a Coke after, but I'll still be home before eleven."

Matthew's tone was casual, yet Priss's maternal instincts honed to attention when he mentioned Cooper's daughter. The Maitlands had only been in town a week. Priss expected to be neighborly, but she hadn't anticipated seeing Cooper every single day or that the name "Shannon" would pepper all her son's conversation. "You've been spending a lot of time with her," she said cautiously.

Between wolfing down two slices of apple pie, the bottomless pit found time for a grin. "Just giving her a little whirl, Mom. Nothing heavy, so don't start worrying."

"I wasn't *worrying,*" Priss immediately denied. "I think it's great that you're taking her around. She had to be lonely, not knowing anyone in Bayville. But you've spent almost every evening with her."

Again Matt grinned. "She thinks I'm cute. How can I argue with a girl who has such great taste in guys?"

"You could fertilize the back forty with some of that ego," Priss said wryly, and then slipped in, "Does she get along with the other kids?"

Matt shrugged. "She's the fastest thing this town's ever seen, that's for sure, but a lot of it's show. You know—city clothes, big talk. Once she quit trying to impress everyone, she fit in just fine. Yikes." Her son glanced at the clock, gulped a slug of milk and forked in the last bit of pie as he stood up. "I gotta go, Mom."

In one fell swoop he carried a rattling tower of dishes, glass and silverware to the sink, then bent down so she could kiss his cheek. "As far as Jason driving—"

"He drives slower than a turtle, I've told you a hundred times. His dad told him flat out that if he got a ticket, he'd never see a car key again. We could probably get to the movie faster if we crawled. Don't worry. I'll call you if I'm gonna be late and I've got my key. Catch the Dow Jones on the news for me, would you?"

Her son had turned into a business tycoon ever since he bought two shares of Mattel stock, but he was still young enough, Priss noted, to bang the screen door and take the porch steps in a single boisterous leap.

From the window over the sink, she watched him stride next door in a hurry. These days Matt was always in a catch-a-train hurry. He'd shot up four inches this past year, taken on muscle and breadth and was completely mortified when his voice cracked. Her son had already mapped out his entire future, so sure of where he was going and what he wanted that he made Priss smile. Nothing in life was ever that clear-cut, but after David died, Matthew had grown up fast, willingly shouldering responsibility and proving his basic good judgment. Priss was hopelessly proud of him. He'd rarely given her any reason to worry.

But she was worried now.

And Cooper's daughter was the cause.

Priss finished the dishes and swiped the brick-red counter, wishing that she could get Shannon off her mind. She'd had several chances to get to know the girl—the last time yesterday, when Matt had ushered her upstairs to see the five-week-old kittens Cleopatra had *dared* have in Priss's bedroom closet. All three of them had knelt on the carpet, stroking the white furballs, Shannon chattering like a babbling brook. Priss worked with teenagers. She never had a problem talking with kids, but Cooper's daughter had tugged some unexpected, sharp emotional cords straight from her heart.

There wasn't a shy bone in Shannon's body. She said anything that was on her mind, her face openly and carelessly revealing every feeling. Her laugh was full-bodied and free. She was so young, so beautiful—and so full of hormones. She chose clothes that deliberately flaunted her figure and she flirted with anything in pants. She was coming into her own as a young woman and exuberantly testing—and reveling in—the effect she had on the opposite sex.

Priss had never considered herself beautiful or even remotely close. But the rest . . . she'd been exactly like that once.

That young. That careless. That unbearably, stupidly vulnerable.

Priss squeezed her eyes closed. So easily, a young boy could misinterpret Shannon's flirting and believe she really meant the invitation in those sultry brown eyes. So fast, the girl could get caught in a situation out of her control. She was safe with Matt. Priss knew how she'd raised her son, and knew from her heart that Matthew would never physically hurt any girl. But no fifteen-year-olds had perfect control of their emotions—or their hormones—and mistakes, sometimes terrible mistakes, happened.

Priss opened her eyes and abruptly realized that her heart was galloping, her pulse as jumpy as if a ghost had just walked in her back door.

Impatiently she tossed the dishrag into the sink. She'd felt a strong emotional draw to Coop's daughter from the start. But it was one thing to like the girl, another to imagine danger where none existed. She'd only known Shannon a few days, for heaven's sake. Priss worked with teenagers and knew that all of them were a bundle of hormones, all of them faced growing-up type problems. She worried about all the girls, but she had no factual basis—absolutely none—to worry so persistently about Shannon when she barely knew the girl.

Shannon's father was a different story. An aggravated frown lodged between Priss's brows.

Coop unnerved her, rattled her cage every time she saw him. She'd rather chew rats than relive the past week. Lord! She'd taken him a nice, neighborly casserole, and managed to drop both the lid and the spoon. She stumbled for an answer every time he asked her a question. He'd waved a hello; she'd nearly backed up in the flower beds. The man hadn't done a damn thing but be friendly. He probably thought she was a prime candidate for filler in a fruit basket. Hells bells, so did she. Priss got along with everyone on earth. Her behavior around him had been exasperating, stupid, inexcusable . . . and utterly bewildering.

Abruptly Priss pushed away from the counter. Bewildering, shmildering. It didn't matter why the man had her tied up in knots; what mattered was that she put a kibosh to this nonsense. For now she had chores to do and a shower to take. But the next time she saw Cooper Maitland, she was going to be as cool as a cucumber and the picture of poise. And that was that.

Cooper clawed a hand through his disheveled hair. The kitchen looked like World War III. Patches of torn up linoleum littered the floor. A puddle of water glistened from under the sink's plumbing pipes. Balefully he glared at the roll of wallpaper hanging drunkenly midair over the counter.

How could a little idle curiosity get a man in so much trouble?

After Shannon had left for the evening, he had wandered into the kitchen, popped the lid on a cold beer and innocently glanced around. The room hadn't been redone since his mom was alive—not because his father didn't have money, because Coop had been sending his dad money for years. His father was simply a hardheaded Dutchman who'd been allergic to change. The kitchen was big enough to skate in—had to be a half mile between the refrigerator and sink. The scarred oak table was more relic than antique. The sink had rust stains, and the pale green and yellow wallpaper had watermarks.

Coop remembered noticing all that. He also distinctly remembered telling Shannon, "So what if the house needed some updating?" Everything was livable. Nothing required immediate repair. They were going to enjoy a long, lazy summer—no work, no responsibilities of any kind. Shannon had burst out laughing—as much as he loved her, his daughter could occasionally be *damned* annoying—but Cooper had been serious. He'd been goal-dominated his whole life. From now on, he was into peace and serenity and the life-style of a decadently lazy wastrel.

He still didn't understand how the mess happened. The linoleum... he'd just wondered if there might be a hardwood floor under the pitted green linoleum. The water... he'd just knelt under the sink for a few seconds, curious how complicated the plumbing system was. And the wallpaper... he'd barely touched it. He didn't know anything about wallpaper. How was he to guess the stuff stripped as easily as a hot woman?

Quit whistling, Maitland. Shannon's gonna laugh her head off. She told you you wouldn't last another week without sinking your teeth into something.

But taking on one *teensy* little project, Cooper assured himself, didn't mean that he was going back to his old workaholic patterns. The kitchen wouldn't be work. It'd be fun. His mind spun with plans—he would need the advice of a plumber and carpenter if he was going to do the thing right, and he'd better snag a woman's opinion for the stuff such as layouts and wallpaper.

As it happened, he even had a specific woman in mind.

His gaze wandered to the window over the sink, and abruptly did a double take. Just because he'd been thinking of Priss, he hardly expected her to miraculously appear. Disarmed by the view a hundred yards away, Cooper leaned on the window ledge with a grin tugging the corners of his mouth.

What the hell are you up to, Ms. Neilson?

He'd seen Priss every day. She'd brought over a casserole the first night he'd moved in. Her attitude had been very sweet, very neighborly. And as distant as the moon. Since then he'd borrowed two eggs and a pipe wrench, begged the name of the local well man and sought advice on the character of the farmer managing his dad's land. In every encounter, he'd been judiciously careful not to look at her sideways. She still jumped whenever she saw him at the door.

He knew she liked Shannon. She was damn near incredible with his daughter—warm, natural, easy and breezy. With him, though, she'd been as strung-tight-reserved as a seventy-year-old matron.

She sure wasn't acting like a seventy-year-old matron now.

From the dormer window on her roof, first her head appeared. Then her shoulders and elbows. The sun was dropping faster than a weighted lead ball, but enough sunlight lingered to shine on her mop of wet, gold hair. Literally wet, Cooper mused. Although he could be mistaken from this far distance, he suspected she was fresh from a shower or bath. Her hair was still dripping. And as the rest of her body emerged from the dormer window, Cooper couldn't help but notice that she didn't seem to be wearing anything but a thigh-length terry-cloth robe...and tennis shoes. His grin widened.

She crouched there a second, hovering just outside the open dormer window. He couldn't imagine what she was doing, but then she awkwardly twisted around and started climbing on all fours. Cooper's smile died.

Her house was a bungalow, the upstairs no more than an attic converted into a loft or single bedroom. He didn't need to see the inside to figure out that architecture. The structure was obvious from the steep, sharp pitch of the roof. Very steep. And dangerously sharp-pitched. For a moment, as she crawled up the rough slate shingles, her robe flapped aside. Her bare fanny flashed in the late-evening sun.

Cooper's eyes riveted on the view of that bare fanny, physically aware that he liked her rump. Her rump, her legs, her eyes, her perfectly proportioned body...and the whole female that came with it. He couldn't remember a woman who had snared his fascination the way Priss did—which, as far as Cooper was concerned, was her own damn fault. Her uneasiness around him had nagged like a toothache; he couldn't fathom what he'd done to rub her wrong. His breath? Body odor? His southern accent? He'd never expected Priss to be chummy just because they'd known each other once, but he felt badly that somehow he may have offended her.

She'd been like a complete stranger. At least until now. Watching her, it struck Cooper that climbing a roof was something the irrepressibly impulsive Priss he used to know would have done.

So she hadn't completely changed. That intriguing, interesting thought only registered in passing. By then, Cooper was banging through the screen and sprinting outside, scared witless that the darn fool woman was going to get herself killed.

"Here, kitty. Here, darlin'. Here, sweetling." Priss's bare knees scraped along the rough edge of the roof's slate shingles. The white puffball with the golden eyes was meowing its miniature head off, tucked in the corner where the chimney met the point of the roof. "I'm coming, I'm coming. I'll get you. Everything's going to be fine."

She'd been in the shower when Cleopatra started howling. Five weeks ago, when the brainless mother cat had opted to have her litter in Priss's bedroom closet, Priss had firmly told Matthew that she was moving them to the barn. Somehow it never got done. They'd been so cute those first weeks. So cute. And so quiet. No trouble at all.

"Here, kitty, kitty. Here, darlin'. Here, poochkin. I take back everything I said. I'm not really mad enough to drown you. You can have tuna fish for life if you just don't fall," Priss crooned, and edged forward another foot.

Safe inside the bedroom, Cleopatra was howling her maternal distress. Ahead, just two more feet, the kitten was pitifully meowing with terror. The combined caterwauling was maddeningly distracting; her knees hurt like blazes; her bangs were dripping in her eyes; and she always had, always would have, a terrible case of vertigo. *Could we talk, God? First, I want to thank*

*you for arranging this to happen when Matthew wasn't
around. As we both know, my son would be having a
stroke. And if you'll just get me through this, preferably still alive and with no broken bones, I promise
that I'll never drive barefoot again. I'll never lose another set of keys. I'll never overdraw the checkbook.
I won't go skinny-dipping in the back pond. I won't go
near another roof. I won't do anything wrong, ever
again.*

Another six inches. Then another six. If only she'd
had the brains to put on jeans first. If only the window hadn't been left cracked open to begin with. If
only she'd taken a few minutes to think instead of
panicking when she saw the kitten stranded so high. If
only...

"Could you use a hand?"

She was just reaching for the kitten when she heard
the humor-laced tenor. The startled kitten promptly
zipped past her outstretched hand, nimbly leaped over
her ankle, down the roof and disappeared right back
in the window. Priss stared after it in disbelief, before, reluctantly turning her head.

She knew who it was, had already recognized that
unique male-timbered voice. There was simply no
fairness in life, she thought morosely. If there was one
person on earth she wouldn't want catching her with
her pants down—so to speak—it was her next-door
neighbor.

Two spokes of a wooden ladder were visible above
the roof line. Cooper seemed to be leaning most se-
curely on the ladder's rungs. His elbows had found a
casual perch on her roof, and his chin was cupped
neatly in a palm as if he had nothing better to do than
hang there. And enjoy the spectacle of her making a

total fool of herself with his heavy-lidded, merciless blue eyes.

She gestured. "I was just...um...saving a kitten." She added, "From certain death."

"I could see that."

"It's just a baby. Five weeks old. I didn't think it could get down on its own. The mother cat started howling when I was right in the middle of washing my hair—I didn't know, right at that second, that it was on the top of the roof. I mean, obviously I would have gotten dressed—"

"I kind of guessed that, too," Cooper said gravely.

She opened her mouth, then closed it. His gaze dawdled from her dripping thatch of hair to her short robe to her tennis shoes—duly noting the way she was plastered tight against the roof—before glancing at the open window where the mother cat and white puffball were nestled side by side dozing. Coop didn't smile, but his lips twitched. And the glint in his eyes was chock-full of humor.

Priss felt that foreign-strange wave of nerves. That aggravating, scissor-sharp edginess she always felt around him. But her sense of humor was never far from the surface, and it was a little late to pull off being the picture of poise. Her clinging hold on the roof lacked all claim to dignity, and he'd seen her conned by a five-week-old cat, for heaven's sake. A rumble started in her throat, and sneaked out in an irrepressible chuckle. Then another one.

As if he'd just been waiting for an excuse, Cooper started laughing, too—a big, roisterous, uninhibited belly laugh, the sound as catching as poison ivy. In seconds they were both sputtering and gasping. When he pointed to the peacefully dozing kitten, it started her all over again.

Eventually she regained control. So did he. There was just a moment's silence. A few seconds, when the brush of a scarlet sunset framed his strong, masculine face, and his eyes met hers. She felt the warmth of his gaze, felt a shivery lick of intimacy from the way he looked at her, but she just couldn't put up her guard and be stiff with him. Not after sharing easy, natural laughter like that.

"I don't suppose," she said darkly, "that you'd be willing to forget that this ever happened."

He pretended to consider, then shook his head regretfully. "I'm afraid this is gonna be awfully hard to forget. In fact, downright impossible."

She sighed, heavily and loudly. "All right, Coop. What do you want? Brownies? Your car washed? How about a fried chicken dinner?"

His grin would have been banned in Texas. "The possibilities for blackmail are endless, aren't they? I can imagine what your son would say if he knew you'd been climbing on the roof in only your bathrobe. And the story would be spread all over town if I happened to mention the incident to Joella—"

She promptly upped the ante. "A lemon meringue pie? *Two* lemon meringue pies."

"Don't worry. I promise that I can be had. But since it may take a while to negotiate terms, we'd better get you down from there first. You've got vertigo pretty bad, don't you?"

Priss had no idea how he'd figured that out. Truthfully she'd been doing fine while they were laughing. Her throat didn't go dead dry until she looked down. Still, admitting she had a coward streak went against every grain. "I got up here, didn't I? I can get down. Any old time."

"That's why you're clutching those shingles in a death grip, right?"

"Hey, I'll move. Really. Just as soon as you..." She motioned with her head.

"You want me to leave? Forget it. And don't bother telling me to close my eyes. I already noticed that you aren't exactly dressed for company, Shortie, but I think we're just gonna have to worry about embarrassment another time. Trust me, I've seen all the spare parts on a woman before. And if you happened to slip, I sure as hell wouldn't be much help if my head were turned." He cupped his hand and motioned her impatiently. "Come on. Let's just get this done. Then you can get dressed, and I'll make you a nice tall glass of iced tea, and you can sip it on my back porch while I tease you to death. Turn around backward—you're only going to get dizzier if you keep looking down— and head for the ladder, not that damn fool window."

She didn't want to crawl backward with her rump in the air, but Cooper kept talking, teasing her, distracting her. He mentioned something about wallpaper hanging like a drunken sailor and kitchen layouts and how he honestly needed some help. Priss had no idea what he was talking about, and by that time didn't care. She'd done it. She'd managed to shimmy down that horribly steep roof, maybe not with any decorum but at least without falling. Her tennis shoe connected with the metal edge of the eave.

And then she felt Cooper's hands. First on her calves, then her thighs, then clamping on the ridge of her hips, as he guided her to the first rung of the ladder. When she was steady, he let her go, but still flanked her descent so closely that she could feel his warm breath on her nape.

Priss understood that Coop was only trying to protect her from a potential fall. His touch had been sure, steady, supportive, nothing provocative about it. Yet when she finally reached level ground, her pulse was patchy and her whole body felt boneless. She'd been dizzy from the height, she reminded herself. And naturally she was shivery. Once the sun dropped, the evening air had picked up a chilly nip.

She felt even more shivery when she turned and found Cooper was still close. Hovering close. And bent over a little so those shrewd blue eyes could get a good look at her face. "You okay now?"

"Beyond feeling like a total idiot, I'm fine."

He smiled. But he also studied her flushed face, and the way she wrapped her arms tightly across her chest. "You're cold. I'm going to change that order for an iced tea to hot coffee, or maybe a little mulled brandy. What'll it take you to get dressed? Ten minutes? Then you've got a date on my back porch."

Cooper promptly heaved the wooden ladder on his shoulder and headed for his father's barn. He'd hardly given her the chance to refuse, Priss mused, but that was okay. He'd been nice. More than nice. He'd been funny and kind and he'd jumped to help when he thought she was in trouble. If she couldn't totally shake that zoom of acceleration she felt around him, laughing together had helped. She wanted those stupid skittery nerves gone for good. Priss had always faced problems head on. A little one-on-one time with her neighbor might be just the key.

Ten minutes later, her bedroom window was closed, the kittens safely asleep, and she was fully dressed in white jeans and an old navy sweatshirt. She streaked some blusher on her cheeks and crossed the yard to his house with a clipped, confident gait. She was going to be natural with that man—or die trying.

She expected to be a little uncomfortable.

She expected herself to handle it.

But she never once expected what happened.

Three

————

Priss had planned to drink a fast cup of coffee and be back home within an hour. Yet an hour had long passed, and she was still on his back porch, nursing a brandy, her legs curled up under her in an old wicker rocking chair. Coop had chosen to sit on the ground, his back against a white wooden porch pillar and his long legs stretched out. He'd brought out the bottle of brandy, but so far he hadn't finished his first glass yet. He was too busy talking.

Crickets hummed in the bushes. Fireflies danced in the spongy green grass. The moon had long risen, a cradle-shaped crescent backdropped by a black velvet sky. When they'd first come out, Cooper had flipped off the porch light. It was dark on the shadowed porch, as dark as a private dream and just as quiet. A breeding ground for secrets, Priss mused. Was that why she was finding it so easy to be with him?

Maybe it was simply impossible to be wary of a man who was so willingly open and honest. Priss understood his hunger to talk. Everyone had a need to let things out sometimes. But Coop was telling her things that were absolutely none of her business. Things that only friends should be sharing. Things that implied that there was already a wealth of trust and understanding between them.

"I gave Dad money over the years. Hell, I had it to give, and I knew he had some tough farming years. You know what he did with it?"

"What?"

"Nothing. Not one damned thing. Every penny is still in the same bank account I started for him. Never spent one dime, not on himself, and sure as hell not on the house. When I first walked in the door, I couldn't believe the shape the place was in. God, he was a hardheaded Dutchman. And as stubborn as a mule."

Priss said softly, "You miss him."

"Like a raw sore." He shook his head. "We fought like cats and dogs, but the love was still there. I should have come back home—then I'd have realized how he was letting things go. But he always liked to travel, claimed it was easier for him to come visit me than the other way around. The last time I saw him, I didn't like his color. Set him up with a doctor's appointment for a complete physical in Atlanta. Do you think he'd go?"

"He didn't like doctors, Coop."

"I should have stuffed some chloroform over his nose and dragged him there. When Mom was alive, at least he'd listen to her sometimes. Not me. If I said the sky was blue, I swear he'd argue. I keep thinking that maybe he'd still be alive if—"

"No. Don't do that to yourself. I lived next door to him for a long time, long enough to love him and certainly to know him. He'd have fought off a cavalry to avoid going in a doctor's office, Cooper—you surely know that. There's nothing for you to feel guilty about."

He said quietly, "The guilt's easier than grieving."

She understood. "I know. I've been there. I was only fourteen when I lost my mom, but I still remember."

Their eyes met. Silence settled over them like a blanket that comforted and warmed. Empathy shared was awfully hard to pretend never happened.

And suddenly there was a slow grin sneaking out of the shadows. "You're damned easy to talk to, Ms. Neilson. But you sure as hell haven't told me what I'm supposed to do with that kitchen yet."

Priss chuckled. He'd shown her the disastrous mess he'd made in the kitchen. "I'll give you the name of a carpenter and plumber tomorrow." She hesitated. "Are you really planning on staying in Bayville longer than the summer?"

"I don't know. I'd have to ask Joella at the post office. The last I knew she was keeping track of whether I walked, moved or breathed and giving me advice on all three. Assuming I have any say in the matter, though, yes. This is home. I plan to stay."

She reached down with her bare toe and set the rocking chair creaking again. "Small town life couldn't hold you before, Maitland. You don't think you're going to be bored?"

It wasn't a loaded question. Just more conversation. Yet as with every other subject they'd wandered into, Cooper responded by giving her a blunt, honest picture of his life. "About six months ago, I got up one morning, stumbled into the bathroom to brush my teeth and opened the medicine chest for the tooth-paste. Maybe I hadn't looked before. I don't know. But I suddenly found myself staring at this open chest jammed full of pills. Pills for migraines. Pills for in-somnia. Pills for tension. I had stuff for stomach-aches, for eye strain, for back pain. It was pretty damned disgusting."

Priss thought of a man who'd always put himself under incredible pressure. Compassion stole into her voice. "Cooper—"

He didn't give her the chance to offer him under-standing. "You asked me if small town life was going to bore me. But I came home to be bored, Priss. The same day I threw all those pills into the trash, I put my company up for sale. The wheels were in motion to come home long before my dad died. I nearly ruined my life chasing after ambition. My marriage broke up because I was never there. I nearly wrecked my health, lost focus of everything that should have mattered to me. No way I'm going down that workaholic road again. All I want is a quiet life no different than any-one else."

Priss was touched—no, moved—by how openly he revealed his past mistakes. But she was also tempted to shake her head at his game plan for a lazy life-style. With Cooper, it was always all or nothing. He sounded as if he intended to pursue a path of boredom with the same single-minded determination he did everything else. But she'd seen his "little" kitchen project. There was no way he could survive inactivity for long.

"Hey," he murmured, "were you gonna let me talk about myself all night?"

"I was interested."

"You were probably as uncomfortable as hell. It's your own fault for being a good listener, but now it's your turn. Besides, this is the first chance I've had to grill my next-door neighbor on the wild things she's been doing with her own life." Cooper lurched to his feet, plucked her brandy glass from the floor, held it up to the moonlight and discovered it was empty. "How come you didn't shoot me for being a lazy host? So I hear you're a counselor as well as a biology teacher."

"No. I mean, I teach but I'm no counselor."

Cooper fetched the bottle and splashed a little more brandy in her glass. "That's not what I heard . . . and God knows, people have been filling my ears with gossip from the day I arrived in town. According to the scuttlebutt, Marjorie Lamb's the principal at the school—and she's good—but when a kid's really in trouble, she sics you on 'em."

Priss shook her head. "It's not like that at all. Marge is terrific, but you know how small the school is. There's no budget for a school counselor and she only has one pair of hands. Naturally if there's a child having a problem, we all pitch in. I don't do anything special."

"I'll be damned. You managed to fool the whole town that you have a talent with troubled kids? And the kids even talk about you like you walk on water. Managed to fool them, too, did you?" Cooper feigned awe.

Priss had to chuckle. "Are you trying to give me a hard time, Maitland?"

"Hell, no. I'm trying to figure out how the sam hill you ended up teaching. Never mind how you feel about the kids. The last I remember you hated school with a passion.''

Priss focused on the lawn, where dew glistened on the moonlit grass like a thousand crystal teardrops. He was right. There was a time she'd never planned to be a teacher, never wanted or expected to see the inside of a classroom again. No one, even David, had ever questioned her sudden turnaround-decision to become a teacher.

Her reasons were buried deep, far back, in a place she didn't allow herself to think about anymore. For one crazy moment, though, she regretted not being able to answer Cooper honestly. He'd been so honest with her. ''I'm not sure there was any one reason I ended up teaching,'' she said. ''It just seemed to work out.''

''I never pictured you with David Neilson, either. You two were like night and day. In high school, if I remember right, he trailed after you like a moonstruck calf. But you never went out with him. It must have been after I left—your senior year?''

Priss stopped rocking. ''Yes.''

''And once you dated him, that was it? Love at first connection?''

''Maybe it wasn't love at first connection. But he was one of the best men I've ever known. I still miss him. We had a wonderful marriage. Everyone in town knew how happy we were.''

He must have heard something in her tone, something defensive that she never intended, because he stopped teasing. ''I'm sorry, Priss. I wouldn't have brought up David if I thought the subject would make you uncomfortable.''

"Heavens, I'm not uncomfortable." But she suddenly was. Cooper's voice was fluid and warm and seeped in a man's gentleness. It wasn't as if he was issuing an invitation, but Priss sensed that he would listen, really listen, if she wanted to talk. For the second time she felt tempted to do just that, to spill out that her life hadn't been as ideal and problem-free as everyone thought.

The urge disturbed her. She was basically happy, the past long behind her—exactly where it belonged. This unexpected feeling of closeness with a man she barely knew was totally out of character. Abruptly she glanced at her glass, discovered she'd finished the last bit of brandy and stood up. "Cooper, I've really enjoyed this, but I should get home. The kids will be back from the movie any minute now."

"Is it that late? Hell, I guess it is." He lurched to his feet. "Let's do it again."

"You bet," she agreed, and bounded past him down the porch steps. For almost two hours, she'd had a wonderful time. She liked talking with him. More than liked. His straightforward honesty was disarming; he expressed exactly what he felt, and his sense of humor made him incredibly easy to be with. More relevant, a little one-on-one time with him proved to be exactly what the doctor ordered. The skittery nerves had disappeared, banished, she hoped, for good. Enough was enough, though. As if there were an alarm clock buzzing in her head, she abruptly wanted to be home. Alone.

"Hold up there," Cooper said lazily.

She spun around. Moonlight shot streaks of silver in his hair as he ambled toward her. His tall, broad-shouldered frame cast a huge, looming shadow in the moonlit grass, blocking all light on her body, even though he stopped a full foot away from her. "I understand that it's late. But we never got a chance to discuss blackmail terms."

Her heart started hammering. Then relaxed. She should have known the devil wouldn't forget about finding her on that darned roof. "You *could* be a gentleman and forget you ever saw me up there."

He shook his head. "That wouldn't be any fun."

She propped her hands on her hips. "You want some advice on your kitchen. I'll be glad to help. As far as I'm concerned, that makes us square."

"No way, Neilson. I'd have come over begging advice on the kitchen regardless. Catching you on the roof in your bare... knees... is a different thing entirely." Cooper thoughtfully scratched his chin. "Your dad's still a minister, isn't he? And I've met your son, had the chance to talk with him. He seems pretty protective of you. I suspect Matthew would be just plain freaked out at the idea of his mom risking her neck for—"

"All right, all right, you cretin. What do you want?"

"That lemon meringue pie you mentioned."

She had to grin. "Done."

"And a kiss."

Her grin died. "Pardon?"

He didn't move. Not then. "You heard me. Hell, it was going to happen sooner or later anyway. You've been worried about the attraction, haven't you? And I've been damned obsessed with wondering how you kiss. Don't you think we'd better get this over with? Maybe nothing's there, but I figure we're both going to keep worrying about it until we find out for sure."

Of all the sassy arrogance, Priss thought, and almost laughed. God knew where Cooper had come up with such a ridiculous assumption. Her nervousness around him had nothing to do with attraction. She was thirty-six years old, for heaven's sake. She certainly knew when she was attracted to a man, and she opened her mouth with a snappy retort that somehow never got said.

Cooper had moved closer. Slowly, gently, his hands climbed her arms, slid to the cup of her shoulders. She felt the heat in his hands even through her heavy sweatshirt, caught the clean male scent of his skin. This close, he blocked out the view of his dad's house and the barn and the oak tree and everything familiar. Everything but him. Her bare toes suddenly curled in the cool, damp grass. *Run.* The instinct hammered in her ears with the roar of a 747. *Run, Priss, quick, while you still can.*

But her conscience forced her still. There were certain tests in life that Priss expected herself to pass. Nothing was going on here but nonsense. Coop was indulging in a little grown-up teasing. A kiss was no big deal. She'd feel like a fool if she jerked away and made a major fuss over nothing. And it wasn't as if she were *afraid* of Cooper.

"God, you're tense," he murmured. "Close your eyes, Shortie, I promise this'll be over in a second."

He was smiling as he angled his head. His mouth touched down softer than a whisper. She tasted a hint of that hot gold brandy, felt the tickle of whiskers on her cheek and the smooth warm texture of his lips— but exactly as he'd promised, that was it.

She could breathe again.

Home free, she thought with a sense of relief.

The elation didn't last long. When he lifted his head, the lazy, easy grin had disappeared. A frown was wedged between his brows. With mesmerizing slowness, his forefinger traced the line of her jaw. A broody, moody silence stretched between them.

Priss broke it. "Hey," she murmured in her lightest tone, "am I off the hook as far as blackmail? All debts paid free and clear? Except for the lemon meringue pie, of course."

It was as if he didn't hear her. His thumb stroked her cheek. "Either you were really worrying...or it's been a real long time since you had fun with a kiss, Ms. Neilson."

She said swiftly, "I happen to have kissed millions and millions of men."

"Boys. When you were in school."

"I was married for almost ten years. Happily married—"

"Husbands' kisses don't count. Once you're married, it's almost impossible to get in trouble with a kiss. There's no danger. There's no risk. There's no fun. We *have* to try at least one kiss for fun, Priss."

They didn't *have* to do any such thing. Priss took a prompt step away from him, thinking *damn you, Cooper, am I really gonna have to get tough with you?*

He snared her wrists and latched them around his neck, then ducked his head. Truly she had ample time to stop him. For an instant that seemed to linger a century, his face was so close that their breaths intermingled; her breasts disturbingly grazed his chest, and her heartbeat recognized exactly how strong and physically powerful he was.

Fear rose in her; an old familiar fear, as thick as a swamp, murky and dark and ugly. Yet in that endless space of a second, other emotions seemed to claw to the surface. Unfamiliar emotions. Unexpected, unnamed, confusing emotions. When she could have moved, she didn't. And then the chance was gone.

His arms swept around her and he took her mouth as if he owned it. She saw his eyes, not blue in the darkness, but black with the devil's own power. She sensed danger as sure as she breathed, and it wasn't as if that wall of fear miraculously, suddenly disappeared. It was just that she couldn't seem to catch a speck of time to think about it. Cooper, damn him, was having fun. She was forced to close her eyes—looking at him this close made her dizzy—and the night suddenly swirled around her, as if she'd been dipped into black satin. The pressure of his kiss increased until her neck arched and her heartbeat fluttered like bird wings.

She remembered that secret flutter, not like remembering a thought, but as if time had suddenly spun back. A hundred zillion years ago, every kiss had been a surprise. Every kiss had been incredibly wicked, delicious fun. She'd been invincibly young, and God, she'd loved it. Loved life, loved being a girl, loved those dizzy fluttering feelings when she was with a boy, loved all the electricity and danger that a stolen kiss invoked.

Longings, suppressed forever, whispered through her bloodstream. Yearnings, long denied, made her feel as shivery as the girl she'd once been. It made no sense. She couldn't fathom what was the matter with her. She was far too old to kiss as if she were an untried girl, and Cooper... oh, Lord, Cooper. Necking with the boys back then had absolutely nothing in common with necking with a full-grown man who knew exactly what he was doing.

He lifted his mouth, only to trail a hot, wet path of kisses down her jaw and the length of her throat. Her lips burned, stung, from the imprint of his. She couldn't catch her breath. He mapped the pulse in her throat with his tongue, nuzzled the soft skin under her chin. His hands found their way under her sweatshirt and roamed the warm bare flesh of her back, like an explorer on a discovery mission. Her bra catch was in his way. As quick as a pinch, he unsnapped it.

Alarm bells clanged in her mind as loud as a fire brigade.

But he never touched her breasts. And the whole nature of his kisses suddenly changed. He'd been playing, she knew. He'd been having a damned good time shaking her timbers with those lusty, earthy kisses, but that was all that had been going on. Coop just didn't know how to do anything halfway. He kissed with the same dynamite charge he did everything else.

But when his mouth homed back to hers this time, it was different. His tongue stroked the seam of her lips, shilly-shally slow, waiting until she had to draw a breath before stealing inside. Tongues touched tongues, and he pulled her closer, his arms anchoring her to him.

No breeze ruffled through the trees. No cars passed on the country road. In the sudden total quiet, Priss felt something huge well up inside her. His mouth fused on hers like sealing glue, and she tasted desire in his kiss. She tasted need. But more than anything, she tasted an intense and powerful loneliness.

He wasn't playing anymore. He wasn't having any fun at all. As if she had no choice, as if she'd never had a choice, her hands clenched tightly at his nape and she leaned up and into him, taking his mouth as he took hers. Her response was nothing she could help. Nothing she could stop. To hold and be held—she knew that need. Loneliness—she knew about loneliness and soul-dark nights and thinking that no one would ever, ever be there.

He murmured something gruff and low. Her name? And then angled his head yet again. So unreasonably, he kissed as if he'd missed her. He kissed as if he'd found something precious after years of searching. He kissed, as if now he'd discovered her, he couldn't— wouldn't—let her go.

Priss could never remember feeling more connected to another human being. Her senses spun like an unraveling, flowing ribbon. The spin of desire, the unique and fragile intimacy she found with him seemed as natural as her own heartbeat. For a time. Real life intruded in the shock of a minute when she realized that she was on tiptoe, plastered against him closer than butter on bread. Her breasts were crushed flat against his chest and his arousal was ironed against her pelvis. He was hard, aching hard, throbbing hard, and he was holding her so tightly, that the sensation of being trapped slammed through her like a freight train.

A roar filled her ears. An instinctive hiss of panic. A blind rush of terrible, intolerable vulnerability. Cooper was a physically strong man. Overpoweringly strong. And Priss knew better; she *knew* better than to ever get herself into a situation that she couldn't control.

"Coop. Stop."

He immediately lifted his head. His eyes looked stunned, fierce with desire, his moonlit face harsh with intense emotion, and she thought—she *knew*—it wasn't going to be that simple.

But it was. His lungs hauled in a ragged breath. He loosened his clutch on her; his hands gentled, then stroked, then eased out from under her sweatshirt. She still wasn't breathing. She felt like a fawn, frozen in a hunter's spotlight; his gaze focused straight on her face and wouldn't let go.

The pad of his thumb stroked her cheek. "Are you okay?"

She nodded.

"Well, damned if I am. Ever feel hit with a two megaton wattage of lightning?" He obviously meant to coax a smile, but she couldn't seem to find one to give him. Whatever he saw in her face with those dark, searching eyes made him hesitate. "I...I didn't know anything like that was going to happen, Priss."

"It's okay."

"I thought I'd done something to make you uncomfortable around here. So I might have meant a kiss, but I never meant a pass. We're living next door, I was just trying to make things lighter, easier between us—"

"Cooper, it's okay," she repeated.

He was frowning now, and he started to say something else when they both heard car doors slam from the distance of the road. He squeezed her shoulders, as if asking her to stay just another second, but Priss was already pulling free, backing away.

"It's the kids. I really have to go," she said swiftly.
And though she wasn't proud of her fast retreat, she
pelted straight for the house.

Cooper pushed open the doors to Stevens Hardware. The place was beginning to feel like a second
home since he'd been there every day that week. Just
inside was an old-fashioned cracker barrel. Typical of
a country hardware store, the place was jam-packed
from stem to stern, nothing presented fancy or an
ounce of high tech, but it sold everything on earth—
horse feed, ten-penny nails, rabbit cages, plumbing
pipes, lumber.

All he wanted was paint. Matt came galloping toward him out of nowhere. Priss's son had developed
an uncanny sense for knowing when he was in the
store. "Can I help you, Mr. Maitland?"

"I don't want to drag you into this one, Matt. I'm
on an impossible mission," Cooper said dryly. "I need
paint."

Matt eagerly tagged behind him. "That's no sweat."

"I need vanilla-colored paint."

"Beg your pardon?"

"Have you ever worked with women, son? Your
mother claims the whole house will glare if I use plain
white. Shannon said that most off-whites would be too
dingy. Vanilla is the color they both agreed on. If you
want the truth, I don't expect to find a paint that looks
remotely like ice cream—but that's what I've been in-
structed to come home with."

Cooper purposefully made his tone sound ag-
grieved to make Matt chuckle. Man to man, they
studied the paint cards, eventually choosing a shade
that seemed "vanilla" enough. Then the paint had to

be mixed. Six gallons. Enough to do the kitchen, hall and living room—projects Cooper had sworn not to touch until fall. But the kitchen was already torn up, and when it was done, he'd already figured out that the rest of the house was going to look like hell if he didn't do something to brighten it up.

The whole time, Matt kept up a conversation. "You think the last big deal in the Middle East will affect the market, Mr. Maitland?"

"You follow the market?"

"I've had stock for years," Matt assured him. "You don't know how great it is to be able to talk to you. No one in town has any experience in the business world. Not *real* business."

Cooper was aware that the boy had a small case of hero worship. Whenever he was in the hardware store, Matt hovered to help. And at home, he found excuses to amble over—inevitably to see Shannon—but also to talk. Cooper liked him. He just wished the mother was half as easy to win over as the son.

Coop wasn't sure whether Priss fascinated or mystified him, but it seemed to be both.

She'd been an angel of a neighbor. She'd brought over a lemon meringue pie—tart, tart lemon and a three-inch mound of meringue, the best damn pie he'd ever had, and God knew it was his favorite. She'd also brought him a tobacco-chewing, whiskered, emaciated guy named Studge, who spoke in grunts, had completely torn up his kitchen, and—as Priss had promised—was the best carpenter Coop had ever seen. She'd talked colors and layouts with him. She'd talked counters. She'd sat next to him in church on Sunday, while her dad preached the same fire and brimstone threats Coop remembered as a kid, and she'd taken to inviting him and Shannon over for dinner. Coop could cook, but temporarily his kitchen qualified as a war zone. In short, she'd been wonderful.

But, for her, it was as if the embrace they'd shared had never existed.

Cooper couldn't shake the memory of that embrace. But he didn't want to shake it. The picture of Priss was lodged in his mind . . . the look in her eyes when she caught fire, the feel of her small body coming alive for him, the wildness under all that cool surface. He didn't want that picture dislodged.

His mind was so captured with Priss that for a moment he didn't realize Matt was still talking to him.

"Everybody leaves Bayville after high school. I'm not going to do that." Matthew sealed the lid on a gallon of paint. "I want to go to college, you understand, but after that . . . well, I'd just be another hick farm boy waiting in line if I headed for a big city. Here, I could make a difference. Be someone. You have any idea how many opportunities there are around here, Mr. Maitland—not that I want to bore you—"

"I'm not bored, Matt. I'm interested. What kind of opportunities?"

"Well . . . take Mr. Stevens. He's fifty-five, so he's gonna retire in another ten years. He runs this place like I can't believe. Like I'm only fifteen, and even I can figure out how he could organize this place better, expand the inventory. There's opportunities like that all over town. You know the Eastman family?"

"From a long time ago, yes." The Eastmans were big landowners, the closest Bayville was likely to come to landed gentry. Cooper had gone to school with Bric, played football with him.

"Well, Bric Eastman's got a lot of things sown up around here, from land to property. And I'm not saying that I could be, like, competition for him. Only that there are a lot of things a guy could do if he had some ambition, was willing to work at it."

Cooper wished his daughter had half of Matt's straight common sense and steadiness. Priss had done a good job with him. "Was it your dad who interested you in business?"

"Not directly. I mean my dad's whole life was farming. But he was pretty strict about my getting good grades. Always said that he never had any, and education was the key to bettering myself."

"Put a lot of pressure on you?"

Matt nailed down another gallon. "Not really. My dad was like...low-key, you know. Didn't talk much. But he was there, always around. Anything that flustered Mom, he was like a brick."

"A lot of things fluster your mom?" Cooper asked casually.

Matthew chuckled. "When the chips are down, Mom's cool. If something's really wrong or anybody's in trouble, she'd be there helping out faster than you could spit. But she loses anything that isn't pinned down. She can't add up a checkbook worth zip. I've seen her leave the house for school without her shoes." He added seriously, "She just needs someone to watch over her a little. She gets distracted. God, are you gonna tell her I said this?"

"Only if someone held a loaded gun to my head."

Matt grinned again. "You're okay, Mr. Maitland." He hesitated, then ducked his head for the last can of paint. "Just for the record, it'd be okay with me if you and Mom...um..."

"What?"

"You know. Saw each other some. Like I told her that before. She hasn't been out with anybody since Dad died, and I think that's nuts. I mean, some real jerks have asked her out. I wasn't surprised she gave them the slip. But there are some nice guys around and she sent them packing, too. Never even gave them a try. I probably shouldn't be telling you this, but I just..." He shrugged. "I was just trying to say that with you, I think it'd be different, is all."

Matt didn't come out and say it, but Cooper got the message. He had permission to date Priss. As he loaded the six gallons of paint into the trunk of his Lincoln, he mentally calculated that he'd now accumulated permission slips to see Priss from nearly everyone in town: Joella, the tobacco-jawing, grunting carpenter, Spence Dawson at the drugstore, Babe O'Connell at the Stopaway Restaurant. Even her father—who used to scare the wits out of him with his sermons—had made some obscure comment about how glad he was that Cooper was next door to his daughter.

Bayville was hoping to eyewitness a courting.

They were going to be disappointed. Cooper never did anything in front of eyewitnesses.

But he had to admit that seeing Priss had definitely been on his mind. Assuming that he could ever catch the woman alone, which was proving a tad tricky. As often as he'd seen her, Priss managed to disappear faster than a trained escape artist when there weren't other people around.

A dozen times, he'd mentally kicked himself for scaring her. He knew he'd let a few simple kisses explode into something far more volatile and serious.

But that night, it had seemed right. He'd talked to her more easily and honestly than he could ever remember talking with a woman. Why it was different with her God only knew. She'd listened, he knew that. She understood, he believed that. And when he'd lost his head because she was so damned warm and giving, he could have sworn—he *did* swear—that Priss had lost her head, too. She'd let loose like a flower after a rain, a tight bud suddenly open, wide open, soaking in his touch like a flower thirsty for sunlight.

Cooper was still flummoxed, honestly unsure as to how and why he'd managed to frighten her. Suddenly she'd been shakier than a newborn colt, almost panicky. He felt guiltier than a low down dog for scaring her, but damned if he understood it. As evocative and powerful as that embrace had been, no real physical intimacies had been involved. They'd both been standing, fully clothed. He'd done nothing he knew of to provoke that anxious panicky reaction.

And it had nagged on his mind, like the clue in a mystery, that there had to be a reason why a woman as emotional and warm and passionate as Priss had chosen to be celibate for the past five years. Still carrying a torch for David? Or something more complicated?

Cooper had no answers, only the strong intuition that he'd blundered like a heavy-footed moose into something that was vulnerable for Priss. His blundering in itself was no surprise. He'd bungled his marriage with similar finesse. Possibly a subtle, sensitive man would know how to handle Priss. Regretfully he'd never had a subtle, sensitive bone in his whole body.

His conscience reminded him that he hadn't come home intending to become involved with any woman.

His conscience nagged that to risk hurting a vulnerable woman was beyond unforgivable.

His conscience urged him to do the obvious. Leave her alone.

Cooper sighed. He'd been listening to that dratted voice of his conscience all week.

But damned if he could get her off his mind.

Four

Wednesday nights were traditionally reserved for "girls only" for as long as Priss could remember. Husbands and children were banished; grubs were donned, gossip packed in and an effort was made to overindulge in foods of absolutely no nutritional value.

The usual group of five women inevitably fluctuated in the summer months. Two friends were teachers on vacation, another busy with a little league game, so there were only two of them tonight. It didn't matter to Priss. The evening was blistering hot, which didn't matter to her, either.

For a few hours, she wasn't going to see Cooper, wasn't going to glance even once at the house across the yard, and she wasn't going to allow one single thought or worry about the man to cross her mind.

Nothing could have been easier. Marge arrived at seven, barefoot and carrying a grocery bag stuffed with baking ingredients, and already talking ten for a dozen. An hour later, Priss surveyed her ransacked kitchen with a blissful grin. Bowls and pans littered the counter. Whisks, wooden spoons and beaters dripped from various containers. The whole room reeked of sinful smells—chocolate, egg whites, whipping cream, vanilla and the potent aroma of coffee liqueur.

"Why did I let you talk me into this?" Marge groaned. "Why, why, why? The temperature has to be a hundred and ten, and we're turning on the oven. Does this strike you as insane or what?"

"Hey, don't try to shift the blame on me. You're the one who came up with the recipe for Chocolate Damnation—and brought half the ingredients besides." Priss glanced at her friend, and observed dryly, "Most of which seem to be on you."

Marge looked down and started laughing. When in a business suit, with her wire rims and brunette hair tacked back, Marge exemplified the image of a stern-faced principal. She surely didn't now. Her hair was straggling from a tortoiseshell barrette, and her shorts and loose tank top were spattered with chocolate and dots of whipping cream. Priss knew she looked no better.

"We're going to need a shower before this is over."

"To heck with the shower. Let's just get out of this kitchen before we fry." Marge popped the cake pan into the oven and fanned her hot cheeks. "Have you seen Lainie? She got a permanent the minute she heard Cooper was back in town. Of course, she can't shed that extra thirty pounds quite so easily. You think her husband knows that she and Cooper had a big thing going in high school?''

Priss piled dishes into the sink to soak. One reference to Cooper, she thought firmly, did not mean the man was on her mind. ''Lainie told every girl in the locker room.''

''But that was girl talk. It doesn't mean Johnny caught wind of it. And Cooper never struck me as the kind to kiss and tell on a girl.'' Marge tossed the hot pads on the counter. ''She's never forgotten him, you know. I don't know when they're going to catch up, but I'd sure like to be a fly on the wall. I'll bet he doesn't even recognize her.''

''Meow,'' Priss said wryly.

Marge grinned. ''Well? Do you think he'll remember her?''

Of course he'd remember her, Priss thought. With headache clarity, she recalled all the sexual exploits about Cooper's prowess that Lainie used to boast about. And that was years ago. He'd been young. A novice lover. Priss had sampled exactly how much power he packed in a few kisses now. The man should be licensed as dangerous. A lethal substance when exposed. Technically Priss had gained in maturity and experience, too—enough to know that she was way, way over her head with Coop. It didn't matter if she cared. It didn't matter how much she liked him.

She was smart enough to stay away from quicksand.

Smart enough to keep the man off her mind, too—if Marge would only tune to a different channel.

''Priss? Are you woolgathering or what? I was asking you about Lain—''

"I've never tried Kahlúa, have you?" She diverted her friend by snatching up the small bottle of coffee liqueur. "The recipe only called for a quarter of a cup. I'm stuck with the rest. You want a glass?"

Marge took an experimental whiff. "Good grief. I'm not sure what Gabe will say if I come home with hair on my chest." She grinned. "On the other hand, he's picking me up. I don't have to drive. Let's try it. And then for heaven's sake, let's get your timer on and get out of this heat."

Priss poured two small glasses. When the buzzer was set for the cake, they ambled into the living room, dodging kittens, both choosing chairs close to open windows. All day there'd been a breeze. Not now. Lightning crackled in the far west, but the storm wasn't going to break and cool things down for hours yet.

"Where'd you stash the kids tonight?" Priss asked.

"Overnight at my sister's. And Gabe stopped with a few of his business cronies to shoot the bull at the Stopaway, par for the course on Wednesdays. An evening away from each other does wonders for a marriage. Either that or the beer. One beer and Gabe is *always* in the mood." Marge's eyes twinkled. "Guess who's pregnant again?"

"Who?"

"Janet Eastman. God, it couldn't have been planned. They've already got four, and I wouldn't wish morning sickness in the summer on my worst enemy. Either that girl never heard of birth control or Bric must be one maestro of a lover."

Priss stiffened like a poker.

"What's wrong?"

"Nothing." She took a quick gulp of the coffee liqueur. The taste was thick and pungent and burned all the way down her throat. Then she took another. "Did you end up hiring that teacher you mentioned for the fall? What was his name? Calloway?"

Marge stretched out her long legs, easily coaxed into talking shop. After a discussion of the new teacher, the conversation wandered into curriculums and school budget problems and what might happen over the summer to some of their more troubled kids.

Neither heard the back door open. Neither heard anything until a feminine voice pealed out, "Mrs. Neilson? Are you home? It's just me, Shannon."

"Come on in! I'm in the living room," Priss called.

"It smells wonderful in the kitchen." Shannon ventured through the doorway, hugging her arms, her eyes shy. "I just wanted to ask you . . . if I could get Dad to agree . . . if maybe I could have one of the kittens when they're old enough to give away?" Abruptly she spotted Marge. "Oh, I'm sorry, I didn't realize you had company."

"It's okay," Priss said reassuringly. "Marge, this is Shannon Maitland, Cooper's daughter. And Shannon, this is an old friend of mine, Mrs. Lamb, the principal at our local high school."

Shannon heard the word "principal" and stopped dead.

"Trust me, I don't bite kids in the summer," Marge said with a grin. "We're just talking. You're welcome to join us. I'm surprised Priss didn't rope you in a chair the instant you said you were willing to take one of those ragamuffin cats off her hands."

"I'm not sure my dad will agree, Mrs. Neilson." For a few minutes they chitchatted about cats, but Shannon didn't move from the doorway until the hall light popped on. Matt, who rarely left the male sanctuary of the den on Wednesday nights, claimed he was dying of thirst. He smiled a hello when he spotted Shannon.

Shannon did more than smile. The shy girl hugging her arms disappeared. Her eyes lit up like sparklers. With a toss of her long blond hair, she pounced over to him with a sashay in her behind. Once the two had garnered sodas and chips from the kitchen, they disappeared toward the den.

"Eeek," Marge murmured when the kids were out of sight. "I think a heat wave just passed. Your son looked like he didn't know what hit him. How come you didn't tell me what was going on?"

"Nothing, I hope, is going on." Priss restlessly swung her legs over the side of the chair. "When they moved next door, Shannon was totally new in town. Matt's been taking her around."

"And you think that's all that's going on?" Marge scooped up a magazine and worked it like a fan, her expression full of disbelief. "It's not like you to stick your head in the sand, Priss."

"I know." A white kitten leaped on her lap and nestled into a ball. Briefly Priss wished she could find some nice safe corner and curl up, too. Did every subject they talked about tonight have to indirectly lead back to Cooper? "I'd be lying if I said I wasn't worried about the two of them. But it's Shannon more than Matthew. At least Matt's my son. I can talk to him—and have. But Cooper's daughter...she's just one of the most vulnerable kids I've met in a long time."

When Priss fell silent, Marge pressed. "I heard Cooper was divorced and his ex-wife remarried. Touchy situation? Is that why Shannon's with him?"

"Not exactly. I think it's more like Cooper gathered her up because he saw problems brewing. She's mentioned her stepfather, seems to like him, but apparently she's never been on a wavelength with her mother. She admits to having done some things like skipping school, ignoring curfews. But there isn't a bad bone in her body, Marge. She's just having trouble finding her way. I'm sure the divorce is a factor, but so is her age. And hormones. She simply has more energy than she knows how to control."

"You've thought a lot about her, haven't you?" Marge cocked her head. "And you like her. It's in your voice."

"Very much," Priss admitted.

"And have you thought about Cooper?"

She nodded. "He's really terrific with her. She's just at such an awkward growing-up stage that—"

"I didn't mean in reference to Shannon," Marge interrupted dryly. "I meant have *you* thought about Cooper? You've obviously become personally involved with the daughter of your next-door neighbor. I don't suppose there's the slimmest chance, the remotest chance in heaven, that you've conceivably noticed that the father of that girl is the sexiest man this town has ever seen?"

"Heavens," Priss said swiftly. "You finished the Kahlúa. I'll get you a little more."

Hours later, when the storm broke, the house was completely dark. Everyone had sampled the Chocolate Damnation. Gabe had picked up Marge; Shannon had long headed for home and Matt was sound asleep.

Not Priss.

She stood in the open kitchen doorway, feeling the wind tuft and gust through the screen. Curtains billowed. Lightning clawed the black sky, followed by the rumbling growl of thunder. The first fat drops of rain splatted on the porch.

She ran around closing windows, but within minutes was back in the doorway again. The storm made her feel restless, itchy, as if she wanted to kick something. Preferably her own behind. Even if Marge hadn't relentlessly brought him up, her mind, she knew, would have been on Coop. It had been all week.

If they'd never shared that embrace, she'd be fine. Or if Cooper was even remotely like David. But David had never looked at her the way Coop did. David had never kissed her that way. Her husband had always been careful and considerate with her, the most understanding of lovers. She'd never once felt less than safe with David.

Cooper made her feel as safe as a passenger on the Titanic. He was bold, lusty, earthy. In his arms, she'd felt as if she was on a roller coaster with no brakes. He seemed to take that kind of intense, volatile sexuality for granted. Priss didn't. Priss knew better than to wander anywhere near emotions resembling quicksand, but *damn* him, his loneliness had reached right in and tore at her heart.

And still did.

Priss pushed open the screen door and stepped outside. Rain slashed down. The trees were whipping their branches into a frenzy. Spears of lightning cracked open the sky.

She loved storms. As a child she'd been terrified of them, but she'd mastered that fear by forcing herself to walk in the rain. Even that young, she'd had no patience or tolerance for cowardice in herself. And the lesson had come from experience—when you faced something you were afraid of, the fear lost its power. It always worked.

It wasn't working worth spit with Coop. She'd purposefully seen him every day. Lord, he was a special man. Complex, bullheaded, too smart for his own good, way too tough on himself, funny, honest to a fault, fierce with those he loved. With every encounter, she felt more drawn to him. And with every encounter, those old, blasted fears had sneaked out of her emotional attic and come back to haunt her. Fears that should have been dead and buried. Fears that she'd mastered a million years ago.

Or so she'd thought. So, all these years, she'd believed.

She'd simply have to try harder, Priss told herself. But not tonight. There was nothing she had to handle tonight, and she knew a sure cure for a restless, unsettled mood.

Without another thought, she peeled off the porch. It had to be past midnight. There wasn't a light on anywhere in sight, and the sweet, warm rain drenched her in seconds.

Cooper was poring over a proposal from the Planning Commission when the lights flickered and then went out. The storm had finally broke, he thought, and abruptly realized it was past midnight—and that he'd been sitting at a desk for more than three hours.

All week, mail had arrived by the ton. Ron Shaffer had sent him the Commission proposal. One of the directors at the local co-op had sent him a thick sheath of information. A local realtor had details about a dozen properties for sale. Redd Adkins, at the bank, seemed to assume he would want to know about business opportunities in the area.

Cooper couldn't understand it.

People just refused to believe that he wanted to be lazy. Possibly, like an alcoholic craving a drink, he'd thumbed through those files with his mind revving like a high speed engine. But that didn't mean he wanted work. It didn't mean that he needed to work. He'd just been . . . looking.

And the temptation to *do* anything blessedly disappeared when the lights went out. Hearing the sound of driving rain, Coop unfolded himself from the desk chair and started closing windows, first upstairs, then down. Shannon never heard him bumbling with the window sash in her room. She'd always had the ability to sleep through anything. On a night like this, Cooper couldn't sleep at all.

Negotiating the construction debris in the kitchen was tricky in the dark, but then he stepped outside. It was pouring like crazy. Shadows danced and played in the gusty wind. Clothes hanging on the line were shaking like Halloween ghosts.

Iowa was known for its terrible weather—floods and droughts, blizzards and tornadoes. But there was no yellow in the sky tonight, no threat of anything as serious as a tornado. It was just a lusty storm. Cooper leaped down a step to the grass, and drank in the freshness. Sawdust and paint smells had invaded the house. The rain felt cleansing and cool on his warm skin. In seconds his shirt was soaked, but he didn't care.

Thunder grumbled in the west, but the storm was clearly moving on. He ambled toward the edge of the yard. Then he spotted her. Priss. Barefoot. Drenched straight through to the skin, her hands in the pockets of her shorts and her face lifted to the rain.

The look of her pulled something quiet and sober and deep inside him. This was the Priss he'd kissed. A born lover, sensual to the core, natural with emotions and feelings. And so damned beautiful that she took his breath.

It didn't surprise him a whit that she liked walking in the rain.

So did he.

Priss knew she was soaked through. She told herself she'd go in the instant she felt chilled. But it had been so sticky hot all day. The rain wasn't warm, but it felt cooling, fresh, soothing. Her tongue flicked out for a taste.

"Priss?"

It was a second before her mind registered Cooper's voice. At first all she saw was a huge black shadow looming toward her, coming from nowhere, and she whipped around, stumbling fast.

"Careful there." Instinctively he grabbed her shoulders to steady her. "Damn. I startled you, didn't I? I'm sorry. I saw you over here and couldn't resist joining you. It's been a long time since I found a fellow lunatic who liked to be out in the rain."

It took another second before her heart climbed back down to her chest and she could smile. "Hey. Are you calling me a lunatic, Maitland?"

He grinned. "That's what my dad used to call me—among other things. Whenever there was a major storm warning, everyone else headed for the basement but me. I was always out in it." His palms gentled on her shoulders, then dropped. She'd come up with a quick comeback, and the fear had quickly blinked out of her eyes. But for an instant he remembered, as a kid, finding a puppy caught in a muskrat trap. The pup had been panicked, blind-sick with fear. The same look had been in Priss's eyes. He kept his voice easy, casual. "You'd think at thirty-seven, I'd know enough to stay away from thunder and lightning, wouldn't you?"

"I have the same problem," she admitted. Awareness pumped through her when he stepped back. His shirt clung damply to the muscular wall of his chest, and his hair glistened in the rain. When his eyes drifted lower, she was conscious of how her body was revealed by her wet clothes. She'd liked the feel of his strong hands cupping her shoulders. She liked the way he looked at her. Liked, even more, the dance of risk accelerating her heartbeat, liked being caught in the dark by a man who never forgot, never let her forget, that he *was* a man.

Yet instinctively, unable to stop the impulse, she wrapped her arms around her chest.

"I've done it to you again, haven't I?" he murmured.

"Done what?"

"You're smiling, then you're not. We're just talking, then suddenly you pull away. I don't suppose you'd be willing to talk about it?"

Priss opened her mouth, but no sound emerged. She'd rather chew rats than talk about it. There had always been a chance that Coop hadn't noticed her jumpiness around him. But he had. And now his gaze held hers, waiting, unbudgeably patient. The rain shivered down, but he clearly wasn't going to move until she answered. "It's just...foolishness," she said awkwardly.

"There's nothing foolish about fear. What I don't understand is if I've done something to make you feel afraid of me."

"No. It was never anything you did, and I never meant to hurt your feelings." She grappled uncomfortably for an explanation he might accept. "I think...it's just that you're so much physically bigger than my husband was. Towering taller, physically broader. And sometimes you just startle me."

Cooper didn't know he was going to say it. He didn't even know how persistently the possibility had been gnawing at the back of his mind. "Did David hit you, Priss?"

The question surprised her so much that she lost the feeling of awkwardness. "Good heavens, no. David was one of the gentlest men I've ever known."

He wouldn't let it settle. "You're sure he didn't hurt you? Ever?"

In spite of herself, she started to smile. "Coop, I'm not some vulnerable teenager. I'd never stay in a relationship two seconds if anybody laid a hand on me. And I learned to take care of myself a long time ago. If some jerk tried to give me a hard time, trust me, I can protect myself."

The rain was still sluicing down, softer now, quieter. Apparently she'd convinced him about David, because the intense seriousness eased in his expression. She caught the beginning tag of an exasperating male grin. "Is this the place where you mention the black belt in judo, Shortie?"

"No belts. I never took it up as a sport, but I've had self-defense."

"Oh, yeah?" He looked her over, and that grin widened. "So show me some of the self-defense techniques you know."

She rolled her eyes to the sky. "No."

"Come on, I'm serious. I'm six-two. Weigh somewhere in the ballpark of two-ten. You're what? Five-two?"

"And a half."

He arched his brows. "I'll have to quit calling you Shortie. I didn't know about that half. But the point is that I'd honestly like you to show me. Exactly what would you do to defend yourself against a man my size?"

"Coop," she said patiently, "you really don't want to do this."

"Yeah, I do."

"Real self-defense techniques aren't pretty. It's not a game. In a real situation, a woman has to do what a woman has to do. It's not like parlor tricks. I don't want to hurt you." She drew a breath, instantly recognizing that she'd chosen a poor choice of words. Coop had challenged-male-ego written all over his face. And a *big* grin now.

"Trust me, I don't break." He cupped his hands, motioning her to come at him. "Come on, Neilson. Show me your moves."

"You'll end up mad at me—"

"There's no way I'll end up mad at you."

"This is nuts."

"Of course it's nuts. Who cares? It's past midnight, no one else is insane enough to be out in the rain, so nobody's gonna know or see."

Priss looked at his face. He wasn't going to let it go. She sighed, heavily and loudly. "Against my better judgment, all right. Go ahead. Come at me."

He straightened. "Pardon?"

"I don't know anything about aggressive moves, only defensive ones. That's what self-defense is, for heaven's sake. So you have to come at me. Like you were seriously going to attack me."

He looked as if she'd suggested target practice on her kittens. "I can't do that."

"You can't do what?"

"Honey, you're a woman. And a shrimp of a woman besides. There's no way I would do anything to risk hurting you—"

"*Maitland,* I know what I'm doing. I'm not going to get hurt, and for cripes sake, you were the one who wanted to do this. Just pretend that I'm a man. Pretend that you're mad at me. Make a fist like you're planning to sock me and then charge toward me. Don't think about it. Just do it."

He hesitated, then obeyed. Although his charge was more like a careful jog, and he raised his arm in more a gesture of hello than anything remotely resembling a threatening fist. Still, Priss thought she could pull it off. She watched him, concentrating, waiting for the instant when his right leg was midstep and his whole body weight was balanced in forward motion.

She hooked his shirtsleeve and yanked, simultaneously jamming her hip in his midsection. The trick was leverage. Using his weight, not her own. Her lack of strength was an irrelevant factor when he was off balance. When she bent over, the natural force of gravity was still propelling Coop forward. Straight over her head.

Priss heard the *oomph* when he hit the ground. The sound was reminiscent of thunder. When she lifted her head, Coop was laying splat flat in the wet grass on his back. Motionless. Eyes closed.

She scrambled to her knees and leaned over him, her hands racing over his arms, up his shoulders. She knew he was going to fall, but he wasn't supposed to fall so hard. Her fingertips gently combed through his damp hair, feeling carefully for bumps and lumps.

It took several moments before she realized that Cooper had opened his eyes. And a second before she realized she was draped all over his chest. His heart was thudding like a steady engine. She saw the awareness in his eyes. But she didn't move.

"You're okay? Really okay?" she demanded.

"I'm fine. Although I sure hope we don't need to go through this a second time." He lifted a hand, feathered his fingers through her damp hair. "We did solve something, didn't we, Priss? You don't have to worry anymore. You know for sure now. You can handle me if I get out of line."

She heard him. He'd actually volunteered for that fall, just so she would feel more secure around him. She didn't know what to say.

She didn't need to say anything. Coop filled in the silence. "I'm near death from pain," he informed her. "I need a kiss to make it better."

She sighed with exasperation for his teasing, but again she was conscious that she hadn't moved. The feel of her breasts snuggled against his chest evoked a secret, sweet excitement...but not the nerves she'd had before. He had proved something to her—something about a man who was willing to go the uncommon mile to prove she could trust him. "This is the second time you've tried to blackmail me into a kiss, Maitland."

"This isn't blackmail. This is desperation. My male ego is in tatters. You've probably broken half my bones. The only thing that could possibly make it all better is a kiss."

"I don't suppose it occurred to you that we should both be committed? It's still raining. We're lying here on the wet grass at heaven knows what time of the night—"

"God, the pain," Cooper groaned.

Apparently there was only one way she could get him to shut up.

So she kissed him.

Five

Hanging over the ladder top, his head crooked at an awkward angle, Cooper slathered vanilla paint in the ceiling corners where a roller wouldn't reach. The muscles creaked in his neck, protesting his contortionist posture. Truthfully his behind was sorer than his neck, but that problem had nothing to do with painting.

It had been a teeny bit humiliating to be thrown by a pint-size elf. But more than worth it. Priss never needed to know he'd had a wrestling title in college. If it would achieve the same result, she could throw him any old time. Daily, if she was in the mood. Hell, hourly was okay by him.

God, when that woman let loose, she let loose.

The taste of chocolate had haunted him for days. Not brownies. Not your basic Hershey bar. He didn't know what she'd had, but the barest hint of some rich, dark chocolate had lingered on her tongue. He was probably going to associate that taste forever with the feel of her rain-washed skin, her small cool mouth laying on his, heating up, then catching fire.

Cooper dipped the brush again, aware that he needed to end the whole train of thought. Shannon was painting woodwork across the living room. Studge was grunting and groaning, laying the floor in the kitchen. And Priss was due over. At least, she claimed she would stop by with some wallpaper samples for the kitchen. It wasn't the time or place to be thinking about sex.

But God, she'd been hot. Hot for him. A feather-light kiss had turned into a dozen hungry, winsome, lonely kisses. Her small breasts had tightened, rubbing against his chest. She'd touched his face, and then she'd pushed her hands in his hair and just kissed him. Again and again.

When she lifted her head, he'd never seen a woman look so shocked at herself, so confused. He was neither shocked nor confused. He could have taken her there in the grass without a second's qualm, and damn the rain. He'd found her. That's all he knew. He hadn't been looking, had never expected to find a woman who fit him, who made him aware of why he'd been restless and of everything he'd been missing. He'd told himself he was blinded by passion, and that was surely true. He'd never expected that either at his age and experience—to find a woman who could make him rock hard, hurting hard, in seconds, as if he'd die if he couldn't have her.

God knew why Priss had kept that natural sensual nature locked up for so long. He needed that answer. Her nervousness around him and her admitting that his size intimidated her, had implied to Cooper that some man had physically hurt her. A big man. Yet her husband, though he'd had a muscular build, had never been remotely tall, and she talked about David as if he were some saint. No answer there.

Cooper wished he could shrink. Unfortunately, that not being an option, he figured that trust would take care of the problem over time. She would trust him once she knew him, really knew him, and he'd be careful with her. He'd be patient. He'd go very, very slow....

"Dad?"

He angled his head around the side of the ladder. A thick knot of paternal love lumped in his throat. Shannon was sitting on her knees, a paintbrush dripping on her cutoffs, her hair yanked back in a scrappy ponytail. No eye paint. No five-inch dangly earrings. Cooper had no illusions that he could change that looking-for-trouble temperament overnight, but they'd been talking; he'd been working with her. These past three weeks had been good for both of them. Then, of course, she opened her mouth.

"Did you hear about the Dutchmen who formed a carpool?" She waited before delivering the punchline. "They met at work."

Cooper groaned. "How many more of these are you gonna pull on me? And I don't think that was originally a *Dutch* joke."

"But you're Dutch, Dad. And that makes it so much fun. Did you hear about the Dutchman who got fired from his job at the M & M factory?"

"Please don't tell me the punchline to this. Please."

"He was throwing out all M & Ms that had W's on them.

Cooper groaned again. "Do I harass you with blond jokes? Do I?"

"I don't mind blond jokes. What do you call a brunette guy sitting between two blond guys? A translator."

The back door slammed. A throaty feminine alto called out, "Anyone home?"

"In here, Priss. For God's sake, hustle in here and save me."

Priss turned the corner, carrying a heavy armful of wallpaper sample books. She was wearing white jeans that cupped her fanny, a red blouse with the collar tipped up and red button earrings in her ears. She looked fresh and cool and sassy. His jeans suddenly fit chafingly tight. He had the bad, bad feeling that his resolution about going slowly, carefully and patiently wasn't worth spit.

She took a long dawdling look at the living room, then at him, before shaking her head at Shannon. "He *relaxes* really well, doesn't he?"

"Hey."

Shannon giggled. "I told him he'd go stir-crazy with nothing to do, but what do I know? I'm just a kid, right?"

"Hey," Cooper repeated in his most wounded voice. Priss ignored him.

"The kitchen's in shambles. Now I see tarps all over the downstairs. Studge tells me that he's bought some lumber to make a deck off the back bedroom. I understand the whole house is getting rewired—not enough juice to set up some fancy computer equipment, which he undoubtedly wants for more *play*. Poor baby, is there anywhere in the whole house you can go for peace and quiet?"

"What did I ever do to get picked on like this?" But Cooper couldn't hold back a grin. It was new, Priss's feeling the freedom to tease him. He loved it.

"I have the upstairs," Shannon told her. "Didn't I tell you about that? When we got here, Dad took the downstairs bedroom and gave me the whole upstairs. He said four bedrooms and a bath should be enough space to spread out my female paraphernalia without him having to see it. That's why I thought he'd let me have the kitten. Because I could keep it upstairs and he'd never even have to know."

"What is this? A conspiracy? This is the first I've heard about any kitten."

"It's white, Dad. Gold eyes. All fluffy and soft. You'd fall in love if you saw her. I just know you would."

"I think I've met that particular kitten." Cooper's eyes locked on Priss. "It's a hellion."

"Dad! It's just a baby!"

"*Now* it's just a baby. Kittens have a rotten habit of turning into cats. And if you go back to school in Atlanta, what am I supposed to do with this cat?"

"She'd keep you company." Shannon hesitated. "And anyway, I'm not sure I want to go back to school in Atlanta. Maybe I'll stay here."

Cooper rubbed the back of his neck. Assuming he could get Denise to agree, it was exactly what he wanted, Shannon with him. "We'd have to talk that over, Shannon. Seriously talk. And your mother would have to be included in that decision..."

The telephone rang. His daughter bounced to her feet, and came back from the line moments later with dancing eyes. "Some of the kids want to go riding. Can I go?"

"Sweetheart, you've never been on a horse in your life."

"But I always wanted to. And Matt'll teach me. And Julie says the horses are really gentle. Come on, Dad."

"Maybe. If I get a phone number first. And I'd want to know exactly what time you'll be home..." Shannon was already flying upstairs to change clothes. Short of five minutes, she flew back down, peeled out a phone number and was already banging out the back door.

Cooper climbed down from the ladder. "Maybe we can trade," he said deadpan to Priss. "You can have my whirlwind who throws me a curveball every time I turn around. And I can have your nice, steady, intelligent, responsible son."

Priss chuckled. "Matt thinks you're the coolest thing that ever came to town. If he quotes you one more time, I'm probably gonna smack him."

That made him chuckle. "Well, Shannon thinks you're the most *real* person she's ever met. She's even forgiven you for being a teacher. You're about as near godlike status as you can get."

"Cooper?"

"Hmm?" He saw her take a quick breath.

"You seem fond of my son, and heaven knows I'm crazy about your daughter. But I think the pair of them together are headed for trouble. I've been worried."

"All right. Let's talk about it." He glanced down at his paint-spattered clothes, then up at her ruefully. "But not yet. I need a few minutes to clean up, and let's get those wallpaper samples out of the way."

Priss never planned to stay for more than a short visit, yet two hours later, she still seemed to be with him. Studge, the carpenter, had long gone home. Cooper had only disappeared for a few minutes to shower and change into clean jeans and a plaid shirt, but then he'd headed outside to pull a battered old picnic table under the shade of the white oak. He'd laid out the books of wallpaper samples, then showed up with a plate of cold cuts, fruit and wedges of bread and cheese. He claimed she had to stay for dinner because *he* was ravenous, and eating inside was impossible because every damn room in the downstairs was torn up.

They hadn't talked about the kids yet, but only because he wanted to get the wallpaper decision over with. After mounding a plate for her with food, he'd straddled the seat next to her and thumbed through the pages she'd marked.

That was as far as they'd gotten. "Maitland, you're close to hopeless." Priss reached for a succulent strawberry. "You have to try harder than this. Every time I show you something, all you say is 'sure.'"

"They all look okay. What do you want me to say?"

"You're supposed to tell me what you like!"

"But you didn't tell me this was gonna be so hard." He shook his head in masculine befuddlement. "Plumbing fixtures, I understand. Electrical schematics, laying the project out, costs, that whole part of it was fun. But border trims and teapot patterns. Shortie, this is more intimidating than an audit by the Internal Revenue Service."

He made her laugh. Again. Sunlight filtered through the oak's leafy branches. A capricious breeze feathered over her skin, as mischievous as the look in Cooper's eyes. Priss thought helplessly that she didn't understand. How could it be this easy to be with him?

Something had happened to her that night in the rain. Maybe there was insanity back in the family that she didn't know about? Maybe she had a unique physical reaction to four sips of Kahlúa and a slice of Chocolate Damnation? Because it wasn't her. It couldn't possibly have been her, shamelessly climbing all over Coop, pelting him with kisses, rolling in the wet grass in the rain as if in that instant of time, there was no one else but him. And her. And a sweet hot madness burning her up from the inside out.

Only sweet, hot madness wasn't her style. Coop had gone the long mile to earn her trust, but trust alone didn't begin to explain what was happening to her. She'd trusted her husband. Completely. Pangs of disloyalty and bewilderment troubled her every time she thought about David. As much as she'd loved him, she knew their relationship had never touched these waters. David had always been serious. Cooper had a disgraceful, irreverent sense of humor, and no man had ever teased her the way he did. No one had ever made her feel like just being with him was a champagne high. No man had ever made her feel special. Unique. And as if the growing closeness between them was as natural as breathing.

Even the subject of the kids, which had taken her tons of nerves and courage to even bring up, ended up open and easy.

"Come on. Keep me company while I cart this stuff to the kitchen." Cooper started piling plates and silverware. "It's about time we got off the impossible problem of wallpaper, anyway. You wanted to talk about the kids. I'd have to be deaf, dumb and blind to pretend I didn't know why you're worried. And damned if I ever imagined saying this about my own daughter, but we might as well get it out on the table. You're afraid that Shannon's going to seduce your son, right?''

As Priss carried in the glasses and stray napkins, she quickly glanced at his face. He'd made an effort to make the question sound humorous, but she knew it wasn't a humorous subject for him. "I'm worried about them getting sexually involved, yes. I think they're too young. But it isn't just that." She hesitated, then forged on. "Coop... whether it was Matt or some other boy, I'd still be worried about Shannon. She sends out a lot of sexual vibrations. And she appears much more confident than she is. I'm afraid that sometime, somewhere, she could invite something that she doesn't really want, and be in over her head before she realized it.''

"Believe me, I'm afraid of the same thing." Working around a sawhorse and a half-laid floor, Cooper collected the ingredients to make a fresh pot of coffee. Once it was brewing, he leaned back against the far counter and faced her.

"My theory as a parent was to give her a lot of rope—mostly because my dad gave me none. You put a noose too tight around a kid's neck and they naturally rebel. That's what I was trying to avoid, but the net result is that it's my fault she's wild. She was always like me, not Denise. Denise is sweet and soft. Shannon just drives right over her." Cooper dragged a hand through his hair. "I messed up, Priss. After the divorce, I didn't spend enough time with Shannon. Denise tries—I'm not criticizing my ex-wife—but they've never been on the same emotional wave-length. I should have stepped in a long time ago. Unfortunately that's water over the dam.''

Priss wrapped her hands around the mug of coffee he handed her.

"As far as her relationship with Matt . . . from my viewpoint, I think it's the best thing that could happen to her," Cooper continued. "He's steady, she's flighty. He's thought about his life, goals, has his head screwed on straight." Cooper arched an eyebrow. "Truthfully I was a little startled when he first started quoting Dow Jones to me—"

"Two shares of Mattel stock," Priss murmured.

"Two shares, hmm?" He chuckled, but then he cocked his head seriously. "I think your son is helping. She quit wearing those tops that fit like cellophane. She quit swearing. I see her making good changes. But I've also caught them in a clinch."

"So have I."

Cooper sighed. "I think she's still innocent. But only by the hair of her teeth. I know exactly what she knows about sex because I told her, but damned if I know what the answer is here. If you think it's the right thing, I guess I could forbid her to see Matt."

Priss shook her head. "That wouldn't work, Coop. We're living next door. There's no way they could totally avoid seeing each other. And that's not what I'm asking. I *like* your daughter, and there are ways she's been good for Matt, too. I'm just worried that they've become close faster than the speed of light."

"Priss . . . would you be willing to talk to her? I'm not copping out. She's my daughter. I *want* to tackle this with her, but I sure as hell don't know how a young girl feels. From me, it's father to daughter. From you, it would be one female to another."

Priss hesitated. "If you want me to, I could try."

"I want you to."

She felt easy, relieved. It wasn't that she thought the problem with the kids was instantly resolved, but it had helped to share it, to know they could talk about the same concerns. Coop hadn't become defensive about his daughter like he could have; many parents did, denying any problem until it was too late. Teenagers, too, could develop outstanding skills to hide problems from parents. Priss knew that well. Too well. It was partly why she'd felt a sympathetic draw to Shannon from the beginning.

So many thoughts mulled through her mind that Priss wasn't aware that the kitchen had gone silent until she glanced up. Cooper was still leaning against the counter, one leg cocked forward, the heels of his hands resting back against the counter. A cardinal hopped on the window ledge. Somewhere a truck horn blared. She noticed only him, saw only him. His gaze was lanced on her face as if he'd been intensely studying her for a long time. "Are we done talking about the kids, at least for now?"

She nodded.

"Good, because they're not the only ones who seem to be getting close at the speed of light." He said gently, "I like you, Priss. I like your smile, your sense of humor, the way you look at life. I like being around you, and I sure as hell like the way you kiss. Am I the only one believing that there's something special happening between us?"

"No," she said. There was no way to deny it. In too many ways, she'd already revealed that she had strong, growing feelings for him.

"I don't play with women, Shortie. If you tell me you don't want the relationship to go any further, now, I won't give you a hard time. It'll just be done. And I haven't any idea where or how far we can take this, only that we're never going to find out unless we try. So unless you give me that 'no'... I'm coming after you, Priss Neilson."

She was standing safe and secure on a patch of new flooring, not quicksand. Yet she felt a shivery, sinking sensation at the velvet-dark invitation in his voice. He wanted her. It couldn't be; Priss felt too unsure of what she could offer him, too wary of the new, unsettling emotions he made her feel. She had to answer him with a no, yet when she opened her mouth to say it, something completely different slipped out. "Coop...I'm not sure. For one thing, we just got finished talking about our two impressionable teenagers—"

"Two impressionable teenagers aren't going to be harmed by watching two adults behave responsibly. Have I kissed you all week?"

She shook her head and caught the slow, wicked curve of his smile.

"Did you think it was because I didn't want to?" His gaze wrapped around her as intimately as a bare-naked hug. "I don't kiss in public, Shortie. In fact, I can't think of anything I want to do to you that includes an audience."

Color streaked up her cheeks. He was moving straight toward her when the back door slammed. Shannon blew in, bouncing all over, bubbling with tales of her riding adventures. Both Coop and Shannon attempted to coax her to stay, but Priss was already jogging for the door. Coop needed time with his daughter. Matt should be home and was probably wondering where she was. And never mind that comical look of frustration on Cooper's face. She'd definitely gotten herself in enough trouble for one evening.

Yet as she sprinted across the yard, she found herself smiling.

At home, Matt wanted to practice night driving with his new learner's permit. Her son had been driving on farm roads all his life; he didn't need much coaching from her. As she sat in the passenger seat, she found herself smiling again.

Later, after soaking in the tub and climbing into bed, she found herself smiling yet again. All right, she wasn't sure of Cooper's feelings and definitely not her own. But she was bewitched, beguiled and crazy about the devil next door. To lose the chance to love because of old shadows and nameless fears was absurd. The past was miles behind her.

For the first time in years, she had the dream. She was young, barely seventeen, wearing a loose white cotton sweater and a swingy powder-blue skirt, her long hair caught in a pastel hair clip. She was so excited that she couldn't sit still, stand still, be still. She'd dated half the boys in the junior class, but few seniors—and never *him*. He'd never given her a second look. She couldn't believe he'd noticed her.

She didn't mind that he took her to a party instead of the movie she thought they were going to. When he started drinking beer, she was a little uneasy, but not that much. He only had a couple, and she didn't want to do or say anything to make herself look uncool. He played football. He was big and brawny and self-assured. There wasn't a girl in Bayville who didn't want to date him, but he'd picked *her*.

He didn't take her straight home, but parked his dad's car deep inside a country farm road. There were no buildings in sight, no lights anywhere. She wanted him to kiss her in the dream. She was all churned up, she wanted him to kiss her so much. Her hands were wet, her knees trembly; she was nervous, laughing too much, talking too much.

And then he reached for her.

It happened so fast. She'd wanted a kiss, but never expected a kiss so hard it hurt. She'd willingly parked, but never expected to be pushed down, pinned down, physically trapped. He was hurting her. His mouth, his hands, his weight. He was hurting her all over. She said no. And then over and over, *no, please don't, please.*

He never put a weapon to her throat, never threatened her life. He just wouldn't stop, and he was overpoweringly stronger than she was. Bile rose in her throat with the burn of acid when she realized she wasn't going to get out of this. The fear was paralyzing, claustrophobic, smothering. She couldn't breathe, felt as if she would never breathe again. Her mind whispered a chant, over and over, somehow she had to live through this; it would be over, if she just lived through it.

It didn't take long. When he was done, her clothes were torn and there was blood. He said he knew she'd been a virgin and she could quit crying because she'd asked for it. And the girl, in the dream, froze in confusion and guilt, because she *had* wanted him to kiss her, *had* willingly parked with him. The whole school knew she had a crush on him.

He drove her home like a good date. When she tiptoed into the house, everyone was thankfully asleep, her dad snoring just like always, her two younger sisters camped on the porch because it was hot that June night. She put all her clothes in a trash bag and tied the string and buried it under another trash bag, then crept upstairs to the shower.

She turned the water on scalding and reached for the soap. Her whole body felt bruised, inside and out. She scrubbed everywhere, then started crying just like a stupid baby because she wanted her mom, when her mom had been dead for more than two years. It was just that without her mom, there was no one she could tell. And no purpose in telling. His family was powerful; no one would believe her word over his. Her dad was the minister, her sisters still so young…they'd all be hurt, humiliated, if it got out in town. She could live through it. No one would know. No one would ever have to know if she didn't tell them. She would just forget it, put it behind her and go on. It couldn't matter if she refused to let it matter.

The water in the shower kept coming down, full force, sharper than knives. She washed and kept washing until the hot water ran cold, and still she scrubbed. She had to be able to put a smile on her face in the morning. She had to act normal for the family, and to do that, she had to get clean…

Priss woke up drenched with sweat, her heart pounding. With trembling hands, she switched on the bedside lamp. It was just after five. She dragged a hand through her hair.

How many years had it been since she'd had that stupid, stupid nightmare?

Cleopatra stuck her head out the closet door, meowing a *prowwr* as if to ask what was up. "Go back to sleep," Priss told her.

But Cleo didn't. Knowing full well the bed was off limits, she leaped on the covers and snuggled her head under Priss's chin as if she sensed her mistress was upset. Priss stroked the feline, her gaze sweeping over the familiar bedroom. It was the only room she'd redone since David died. The stand-up antique mirror she'd found at an auction, the brass headboard she'd unearthed from an attic. The walls, carpet and filmy curtains were all ice-blue. She'd wanted a feminine sanctuary, and why not? She'd never expected a man near the fragile antiques, never thought she'd have to worry about a man's work boots putting dirt smudges in the pastel carpet.

She'd never imagined another man in her bed.

Until Coop. She stroked the cat's thick fur with her eyes closed. *Is that why you had the nightmare after all this time, Priss? Because of Cooper?*

An idiotic question. Of course it was. She'd always known why she felt an empathetic pull to Cooper's daughter. Just as she'd known, all along, why Cooper's physical size aroused old instinctive fears for her.

But that old baggage had been handled a long time ago, she thought irritably. It happened. She couldn't change that, but she'd done what she had to do, put that rotten incident behind her, gone on with her life. She'd kept silent because she had to. She'd been strong because she had to be.

And even after it happened, she hadn't avoided other boys. To do that would have been to let that jerk affect her. She refused to give him that power. Maybe she'd been shaking in her boots, but she'd accepted a date with another boy... a boy who'd been stunned speechless that she'd agreed after turning him down so many times before.

That boy had been David, and she never once regretted that decision. He'd been good to her, good for her. If they'd never talked like soul mates or had some earth-shattering passion, Priss didn't give a royal patoot. David had never asked her why she had those nightmares, never questioned why she was so suddenly determined to work with vulnerable teenage kids. He just accepted her wishes, accepted *her*. On their wedding night, she'd been terrified that creep had ruined any capacity she had to respond. But it had been okay, and later, better than okay. David had been affectionate, never demanding. Priss knew she'd pleased him. He'd told her a million times.

Priss opened her eyes. Her whole life, all these years, had been fine. Ups and downs, hard times, easy times, but overall a steady train. Cooper had changed that. Cooper had aroused a poignant, sharp awareness that no matter how good her life was with David, something had been missing. Maybe the stew had been contentedly bubbling for fifteen years, but Coop had turned up the heat. She'd never felt this level of sexual intensity with any man. She hadn't known it was possible to feel this soaring eagerness to be with someone, this crazy lightheartedness just because he was in the same room, this beguiling and bedeviling need to know him.

In her heart of hearts, she knew she'd never been in love before. And for the first time, with Coop, she sensed what the depth of love could be.

Beneath the bed, she suddenly heard scurrying sounds. Cleopatra twitched her tail and innocently blinked at her. Priss should have known. Where the mama cat went, her ragtail family was sure to follow. All four kittens clawed their way up the sheets and bedspread.

"Now look what you've done," Priss scolded Cleo.

The kittens bounded toward her, unimpressed with her rebuke, giving Priss no choice but to gather them up and cuddle them. Her heart was beating so hard, so achingly hard, that she could hardly think. The nightmare frightened her. It hadn't happened in so long. She'd paid every price, in guilt and shame, for what that jerk had done. She'd buried the secret so deep that even her own heart shouldn't have been able to find it.

And it *was* buried, she told herself. The nightmare was just a fluke. There was no reason why she couldn't reach out to Cooper. She needed to be careful not to hurt him. They both needed to take care about pursuing any relationship in front of the kids. But she was a grown, adult woman. Was she supposed to be alone for the rest of her life? Surely she had a right to love and be loved?

What happened all those years ago, she promised herself, had no power to affect her now. She wouldn't let it.

And Cooper would never know.

Six

By Sunday, Priss had put that nightmare in a mental wastebin where it belonged. It was just a dream. Possibly her involvement with Coop had stirred up those old fears, but what happened long ago had nothing to do with Cooper. He was nothing like that boy, and she was no longer that young, vulnerable girl. She'd worked hard, very hard, to never let the past affect her before. She was far too strong to let it affect her now.

And the proof, she'd convinced herself, was in the wonderful times they'd spent together. She'd been with Coop every day. Hiking, fishing, painting—it never seemed to matter what they did. She felt like a rose, slowly unfurling her petals under the sun's warmth. She was the same woman she'd always been, but she felt like a flower in bloom. How could anything be wrong when being with him felt so right?

The strains of Mendelssohn filtered downstairs from the church. She had no more time for woolgathering. Humming, Priss flipped the cuffs of her peach dress. She'd slipped down early to set up trays with coffee and cookies. Other women from the church would come down to help, but not yet. After the last hymn came her father's blessing, then traditionally people gathered on the church steps for a few minutes to chat before milling downstairs.

The old church kitchen was dim and cool, its layout as familiar as her own. Cookies were arranged, the sugar and creamer unearthed, napkins found. It all took a few minutes. She knew the routine, had helped her dad since before her mother died. She was just plugging in the giant coffee urn when the door creaked open.

It wasn't one of the church women, but Cooper, who stuck his head around the doorway, spotted her and hastily sneaked inside. "Thank God I found you. I need a place to hide out."

In deference to the church service, he'd worn a sport coat and tie. The navy sport coat made his shoulders look broader than a barn beam—Coop didn't need protection from anyone in this life—and she saw the mischievous glint in his eyes. "What's wrong?"

"Lainie."

"Ah."

"Don't give me that grin, Neilson. I need help. I don't know what's wrong with that woman." He hooked a finger at the neck of his tie, as if the tie had been strangling him. "You probably didn't know, but I was pretty close with her in high school."

"No kidding?"

"I saw her in the drugstore last week. Went over to say hello, ask her how she was doing." He spotted the tray of cookies. Priss batted his hand when he tried to reach for one. "The woman kissed me in the middle of the drugstore. For pete's sake, I was just saying hello."

Priss had already heard the story from Joella. "It must be tough being so irresistible to women."

"Would you cut it out? She's out there. Walked right up to me when I was talking to your father. Your *father,* mind you, and her husband was standing right next to her. She runs her hand up my arm and says some fool thing about being *so* glad I'm back in town." He cast a mock-terrified glance at the door. "You have to save me."

"I think that's my dad's province. He's the minister."

"Your dad sent me down here."

But her dad, Priss thought, had no idea how Cooper looked at her when they were alone. His gaze shimmied up her legs, dawdled on the open neck of her peach dress, lingered on the shape of her mouth until a blush shot up her cheeks. Without breaking that look, he reached for another cookie. She batted his hand away, again. "You're supposed to be a hot-shot business tycoon. Surely you can handle one teensy old flame?"

"You don't understand what I'm dealing with. She used to be *nice.* Who would have guessed she'd turn into a vulture? She's a married woman, for heaven's sake, and chasing me all over the church."

"Isn't it nice to be loved?"

Cooper heaved a sigh of hurt and stepped closer. "I came down here, desperately seeking a little sympathy and compassion—"

"You came down here looking for trouble, Maitland. Lainie was just an excuse. Get that look out of your eyes. This is the rectory kitchen. And there are going to be people flooding down here any minute—"

"You smell like peaches," he murmured. "And I need a kiss."

"No."

"I'll go back upstairs and face the barracuda. But not until I get a kiss."

"If you're not going to behave yourself—"

"I'm not going to behave myself," he assured her.

He caught up with her at the corner counter between the trays of coffee and cookies, and swooped down like a wolf hungry for the taste of lamb. She caught a whiff of lime shaving cream, and then the heathen kissed her. First, there was just the silvery brush of his lips, a taste of his tongue and the look of devilment in his blue eyes. But then he closed his eyes. And he deepened the kiss.

She told herself that it was wicked to kiss in church. Yet it didn't feel wrong. Maybe it was that God alone knew her secrets, knew what she'd been through, but she'd come to believe that no honest feeling was forbidden in this house of sanctuary. The feel of Coop, length to length, the intimate awareness of his chest and thighs pressed against her...it was still new, it still shot wild, unfamiliar feelings surging through her blood. But there was more in her heart than carnal emotions. If Coop was Viking size, if she couldn't completely chase away that old fear of being overpowered, she'd come to understand that nothing was

ever going to be small with Cooper. He had huge
needs. Not just sexual needs, but such a hunger to
hold, to touch, to be held, that she couldn't stand it.
Once he started kissing, Coop had a disastrous tendency to forget time and place. He forgot everything.
And she'd once dreamed of feeling this way with a
man, a bond, a cleaving so powerful that how could
it be wrong?

When Cooper finally lifted his head, she felt soft
and shivery from the inside out. He looked at her
sleepy eyes and trembling mouth, and slowly smiled.
"Now look what you made me do," he whispered.
"And in church yet."

"You're blaming me? You have a reckless streak a
mile long, Maitland."

"I think you like feeling reckless, Shortie. I think
you like it a lot."

She never had. Before him. The devil stole one more
kiss before letting her go. When the door opened a few
minutes later, both were separated. Cooper had a tray
of coffee cups in his hands. Priss was reaching for the
tray of cookies to carry into the next room, when she
glanced up to see her dad in the doorway.

Paul Wilson took a long thoughtful look at Cooper, then his daughter. "I was just coming to help.
They're starting to drift downstairs. Mary Lynn would
have come down to help but she got waylaid—her little girl skinned a knee."

"I'm on my way," Priss said swiftly.

"Cooper?"

Cooper had been trailing right behind her, but
paused for her dad, his brows arched in inquiry.

Her tall, austere father—the one who'd been
preaching fire and brimstone from the pulpit for forty

years—politely plucked a handkerchief from his suit pocket. "It's up to you, of course. But if it were me, before I went out in public, I'd probably want to take care of that lipstick smudge."

Priss hesitated in the doorway. Coop, who could probably intimidate a boardroom with a few well-chosen words, turned as red as a strawberry.

He took her father's handkerchief.

It was two hours later before Priss made it back home. After cleaning up at the church, she and Matt took her father out to an early dinner, then Matt needed to be dropped off at the hardware store where he was working until five.

She'd just tossed down her purse and kicked off her heels when the phone rang. She recognized the gravelly tenor right away.

"Before you left me—before you *stranded* me—alone with your father, you might have mentioned that he had a sense of humor."

Priss chuckled. "I thought you knew. That stern, mean look is only his way of keeping little boys behaving in church. After Mom died, he raised three girls, for heaven's sake. You think he could have survived that without being human? And neither one of you came out for quite a while. You must have found something to talk about."

She was afraid they'd been talking about her, but Cooper wasn't telling. "I like your dad," he announced.

"So do I."

"But that's not why I'm calling. Matt mentioned that he had to work. Shannon's off with some girls. The sun's shining. It's hot. And the last I knew, there was a nice cool swimming hole at the back of my dad's property. Are you still wearing that peach dress?"

"Yes."

"How fast can you strip out of it?"

To swim, she thought. He only meant to swim. "I—"

"I'll pick you up in ten minutes. You bring the towels. I'll bring something cold to drink. Sound good?"

It sounded great, until she hung up the phone, ran upstairs, peeled off her dress and rummaged in her drawer for her bathing suit. The one she had was kelly green, a one-piece maillot, older than the hills and as comfortable as an old friend. The suit wasn't a problem. It was exposing that much of her body to Coop that suddenly had her sitting on the bed, feeling nerves gather in lumpy knots in her throat. Nerves that totally aggravated her.

It didn't have to mean anything, that they'd be swimming alone, wearing almost nothing. But Priss was aware that it could.

If it hadn't been for kids and circumstances, she suspected that Coop would already have discovered the freckles on her breasts . . . and probably a lot more than that. Stolen kisses were never going to satisfy him forever. If she was unsure of his long-term feelings, she knew he cared. And that when she'd agreed to pursue a relationship, she'd opened the door to sexual intimacy. Coop was an earthy, sensual man.

He also didn't have a lick of patience, and her palms were suddenly slick. Was she foolish to think it would be right with him? Would he know? Would he somehow be able to tell that her marriage bed had been lukewarm instead of hot, that she'd been better at faking it than making it, that once upon a time a jerk had indelibly taught her the fear of losing control?

Stop this, she told herself. She knew it would be different with him. She was a pinch away from being wildly, uncontrollably in love—emotions that Coop alone had made her feel. And a shameless desire seemed to come with that package. She wanted him. Fiercely, unreasonably. Softly, yearningly.

And as far as this afternoon, for heaven's sake, the man had only asked her to swim.

A truck horn honked below. Faster than lightning, Priss pulled on the bathing suit, yanked a concealing big T-shirt over it, snatched up some towels and sprinted down the stairs.

Coop had chosen his dad's old rusty pickup to drive on the farm roads. The windows were rolled down, the a.m. radio tuned to some twangy, foot-stomping country. He motioned her in with a grin, and within seconds they were barreling off, raising dust in their wake.

Par for the course, Priss thought, she'd emotionally reacted over nothing. Coop wolf whistled and waggled his brows when he saw her bare legs, but his ogling was so hammish that she had to laugh. "Is this an afternoon for lazy relaxing, or what?" he demanded.

Cyclones radiated less energy, but Priss didn't tease him. It really was an I'm-gonna-live-forever kind of afternoon, hot and windy and full of the smells of summer. Catalpa trees bordered one edge of the pond, their big leafy branches tossing in the breeze. Bees buzzed in the surrounding meadow of red clover. Monarchs fluttered around the milkweeds. The pond was silt bottomed and deep; the sun danced on the surface like a thousand diamonds.

In the center was an old raft constructed on barrels, floating free, built in heaven knew what generation. For as long as Priss could remember, kids had sneaked off to the Maitland pond in the heat of the summer.

Cooper barely turned the key before he was leaping out of the truck and peeling off his Atlanta Braves T-shirt. "Better tell me now. Are you the kind who leaps in or one of those sissies who eases into the water real slow?"

"Who are you calling a sissy, Maitland?" She tugged off her own T-shirt. Coop never even looked. How could she not feel reassured? And she barely had a glimpse of his body before he dived, clean and fast, into the cool clear water.

She followed. The water felt colder than a shock of ice, exhilarating, invigorating. She raced him, a lap to the raft and back, then again. She was a good swimmer, but could hardly compete with his power and speed. Eventually she climbed onto the raft and stretched out on her stomach to watch him.

He made her want to shake her head in amusement. Coop swam the way he did everything else, all or nothing. A porpoise on full charge. What he called relaxing would exhaust anyone else. He did long exuberant laps, changing strokes, testing his speed, pushing his limits.

Her skin tingled where the sun dried beads of water and soaked in warmth. A dragonfly wisped by. The hot wind stirred the trees, rustling their branches like cancan skirts. A sleepy, soporific feeling of well being flooded through her.

Until Coop finally tired. When he climbed on, the whole raft nearly tipped. He shook himself like a puppy, making her laugh and protest. He stretched out with a flash of white teeth and an unrepentant grin. Any sane man would have closed his eyes and napped from sheer exhaustion. Not him.

"Are you going to burn? I could swim back to shore—there's some sun cream in the truck."

She shook her head. "I'm fine." It was late enough in the day, and clouds were passing in the wind. A sunburn was no real threat, but the burn of another kind might be.

It was there again, seeping into the hot, sleepy afternoon. Desire for him, as sharp and unexpected as a surprise. Yearning, as sweet as a secret. Water glistened like crystals in the thatches of dark hair on his chest. He had an innie for a belly button. Muscular long thighs. Big feet. *Huge* feet. He'd been underwater so quick that she hadn't really seen his bathing suit. It was a disgrace, a bit of navy blue nothing, not tight in the sense of being too small, but what she would expect a man to wear who was comfortable with his body and his sexuality.

The sun peeked, then hid, behind a cottonball cloud. Her skin felt cool, then too hot. Naked, or nearly naked, Coop radiated virility and strength and a Viking set of muscles. She could feel nerves building, but not those awful, anxious kind. Anticipation thrummed through her pulse. Honest, basic, sinful anticipation. They were alone, uninterruptedly alone, for the first time in a long while. Coop had propped up on an elbow. He hadn't seemed to notice her suit before.

But he was noticing it now. And the body in it. His gaze meandered up her legs, her fanny, the long curve of her spine. Her breasts were flattened out from laying on them, the swell pushed above the modest neckline. He was going to touch her; she could see it in his eyes. He wanted that suit off her. He wanted bare skin against bare skin, and the look in his eyes was as intimate as a stroke of fire.

Now, she thought. He lifted a hand and she thought, *now, please...I want to know you, Coop...and I need to know it's going to be all right, and maybe I'm a little scared but there's no way I don't want you to touch me...*

His fingers feathered through her hair, lifting the short strands for the breeze. The caress was gentle, affectionate, even possessive. But not at all what she'd been expecting. "Can I ask you a nosy question, Shortie?" he murmured.

"Sure." His hand drifted to the curve of her neck. A brush of knuckles, ticklish light. Evocative.

"How are you financially set up?"

Her heartbeat skidded to a halt. Money? She was shivering all over and he wanted to talk about *money?* She swallowed a gulp and tried, quickly, to tune her mind to a different channel. She'd die if he realized she was turned on like an overlibidinous adolescent when he obviously wasn't in that kind of mood. "I'm financially set up fine," she said.

"If you happened to be in trouble...like a little overdrawn at the bank for instance...would you tell me?"

"Oh, God. You've been talking to my son. I'm going to kill him."

"Matt never said a word. I'm just asking you a theoretical question."

"No, you're not and yes, he did." She rolled her eyes in embarrassment, then confessed. "I have a teensy problem remembering to add up my checkbook. They all know I have that teensy problem at the bank. But I'm solvent, Coop. Which they know, too."

"The grapevine is under the impression that both your younger sisters regularly hit you up for money. And you're a single mom, making it on a schoolteacher's salary."

"Good grief." She thought, Joella must have been holding envelopes up to the light again. "My youngest sister Leigh just moved to California and is having a tough time getting started. And Faith...she and her husband have two young kids. They both just needed a little temporary help. And I'm fine. I sold the farm after David died, all but the house and fifteen acres. There was a lien on the farmland, but we had good insurance. It was enough to pay off the debts and level the mortgage. Matt and I aren't exactly on a Cadillac budget, but we're doing okay." She looked him square in the eye. "Better than you are, I expect."

"Pardon?" Cooper looked startled.

He'd brought up the dratted subject of finances. She hadn't. All this time she'd kept quiet, careful not to pry, unsure how Coop would react if she said something he didn't like. But didn't she have to know sometime? "Money is a problem for you," she said quietly.

Sunlight put a squint of amusement in his eyes. "Don't you listen to the gossip in town? The last I heard, I was rolling in my multimillions."

"I don't know or care what the size of your bank balance is, Coop. I mean that money is a problem for you at a different level. You like to make it. And that's not a criminal offense. Neither is ambition."

He frowned. "I told you how it was. I thought you understood. I damn near ruined my life on the bandwagon of ambition. There's no way I'm going down that road again."

She didn't contradict him. She just said, "You weren't back home a week before you were tearing into that house. But that's going to be done in a few weeks, and then what? You're nuts if you think you're relaxing. You're as restless as a loose cougar. I don't think that's going to get better until you settle down and focus on something you want to do. This illusion you're carrying around about spending the next years twiddling your thumbs with your feet up is worth horse patooties."

"Ah . . . Shortie?"

She squeezed her eyes closed, thinking, oh God, she'd offended him if not made him downright angry. Why hadn't she kept her mouth shut? "What?"

"Are you by any chance trying to give me a hard kick in the behind?"

Strangely he sounded delighted with her, not annoyed. And when she popped open her eyes, he looked as thrilled with her as if he'd just discovered a rare treasure. Completely confused, she rambled on. "Heavens, no, Coop. I was just trying to encourage you to talk it out. You're having a hard time reconciling it, aren't you? The enormous energy you have. With the fear of repeating the old workaholic mistakes. And I understand that can't be an easy balance for you to find."

He didn't seem to be listening. "People have been yes-siring me for years. Nobody talked back. Even if I was acting like the wrong end of a mule, nobody tried giving me a kick in the behind. Except for you. I thought you were afraid of me, Shortie."

"I...um..." Priss recognized that in some confounded way she seemed to have passed a test. And she saw him raise his hand. She anticipated another affectionate gesture—like the last one, or the one before that. Coop did like to keep in physical touch.

She did not anticipate that he would use that hand to roll her on her back. Or that his mouth would be leveled on hers while she was still wide-eyed with bewilderment. Maybe he rewarded all women who talked back with kisses. Maybe he'd fallen off his rocker.

And then she had the crazy sensation of free-falling. Skydiving from way, way above the clouds. That first kiss wasn't a single copy. And Cooper wasn't wasting time coming up for oxygen. She'd been so sure he wasn't in the mood.

Cooper could have told her. Anywhere near her, anytime, anyplace, he was always in the mood. He'd never limited their contact to stolen kisses just because of circumstances or kids or timing. He simply didn't want those nerves of hers back. Step by step, like ladder rungs, he'd tried to build trust with her this past week. Easy kisses had turned rougher, deeper. Then evolved, so carefully, into embraces that included body contact. Then today, she'd been willing to be alone with him, near naked in bathing suits. And when she'd taken him on in that scrap of kelly-green maillot, Cooper had felt the leash on his control slip loose. If he still didn't understand the nature of the beast that frightened Priss, she sure as hell wasn't as scared of him as she once was.

He'd been good.

At least as good as he knew how to be.

But damned if the woman didn't incite him to be as bad as he really wanted to be. Her small mouth yielded under his, tasting sweet and tempting, tasting like a drug he couldn't get enough of. He eased closer, careful not to crush her, not to expose her to his full body weight, but close enough that he could nudge his left leg between hers.

She murmured his name, making a purring sound similar to one of her kittens. She liked the furred texture of his leg rubbing against her sleek smooth skin. He edged down a strap of her suit, then sank kisses in the hollow of her collarbone, then lower, where the rim of her bathing suit material draped the swell of her breasts. Her skin was warm, dried by the sun. And soft. Like moonshine and silk.

He peeled down the fabric to expose one small, white, taut breast to the sun. And to his eyes. *His,* he thought, and lapped a swollen nipple with his tongue, then nuzzled the plump flesh around it with cherishing, treasuring kisses. He found a trio of freckles. Kissed those, too. He did nothing that could possibly scare her. His only intent was to arouse her.

Preferably to arouse her clear out of her mind.

God knew, he was aroused out of his.

The raft shifted in a strong tuft of wind. The breeze ruffled the blanket of crystals on the surface of the pond. All he knew was her mouth, her skin, her response to him. No woman had ever responded to him the way Priss did. There were no shadows when she was turned on. There was just him. That was how she made him feel, as if all her five senses were on fire and she had a sixth sense tuned just to him.

Restless, she bucked toward him. He didn't let her. Still kissing her, his hand glided down her ribs, her side, the sweet tight curve of her hips. His kisses roughened, deepened, testing. Fires orange hot heated to blue hot. She liked rougher kisses. She liked the sweep of his tongue, the feeling of possession. He stroked her hip, then shifted, slowly to the intimate mound between her legs. She tried to catapult toward him again.

He caught her hand, laid it on his chest, then moved it down his body, slow, around his ribs, slow, getting-to-know-him slow, down his abdomen. His knee tucked tighter between her legs. She clamped around him, impatiently, restlessly. She wanted a ride, his sleepy princess, and God he wanted to snapshot her now, her eyes full of yearning, her mouth softer than petals, her response to him dazzled and bedazzling. Priss liked her pleasure. If she hadn't known it before, she was hopefully learning it now. And he had visions, hot blatant visions, of how demanding a lover she could be, would be, when she discovered how much power she really had over him.

That vision nearly took him over the edge.

For a second, he knew he could take her, that she wanted it, that she wanted him. But that blur of a second contained the last morsel of control he had. And he wasn't sure—he wasn't sure at all—that Priss could handle him out of control.

"Coop..." When he so abruptly stopped kissing her, she didn't know why. He edged the strap of her suit back up her shoulder. She didn't understand. She lifted a hand to touch him, and he grabbed her wrist,

manacled it, until she went still. The hard boards of
the raft, the sharp beating sun, the fretful wind...she
didn't care. Her whole body was throbbing like a
toothache. "What's wrong?"

"Nothing." He murmured low, "If anything were
more right, I'd go out of my mind."

His heart was beating harder than an overheated
engine. His whole body was tense, and she saw his lips
clamp together. "I did something wrong," she immediately assumed. "I haven't...done anything since
my husband died, Cooper, and I—"

"Shortie, you're the sexiest, most sensual woman
I've ever known, ever met, and you couldn't do anything wrong in this lifetime. Not with me."

She took in a breath. Her head fell back on the
muscled flesh of his arm, looking at him, still not understanding. "I...if the reason..." She stopped. "For
the past few months I've been taking the pill. Not for
birth control. I had no thought that I'd need birth
control. It was a regulatory thing, temporary, balanc-
ing hormones. But if a lack of protection was the reason you stopped—"

"Honey, I bought protection the first night I kissed
you. That's how long ago I knew we were going to
make love." He said quietly, "I stopped because
you're not ready."

"Ah...Coop?"

"Hmm?"

"Did you need an engraved invitation? I would
never have gone this far—I would never have teased
you—if I didn't know where we were headed."

His mouth curved in a slow smile. He stroked her
cheek. "I think you like teasing me. And I sure as hell
like being teased. By you. But when we make love,

Shortie, it's going to be all or nothing and no turning back. When's the last time you plunged off a pier into deep water?"

"Maybe," Priss said, "I'm willing to take that kind of risk."

"Soon, I hope, you will be."

"Maybe," she persisted firmly, "I'm a grown woman. A grown, independent, self-supporting woman who's been married, who does *not* need a protector or rescuer, who can even decide for herself what risks she wants to take."

Cooper cocked his head, searching her face, unsure what he'd done to make the liquid fire in her eyes cool down so fast. "I seem to have dug up a touchy bone. You're mad at me?"

"Of course I'm not mad at you," Priss snapped. "I never get mad at anyone. Everyone who knows me could tell you that I don't even have a temper."

"No kidding?" he murmured.

"I just think we should get this straight. *If* we make love, Maitland, it isn't just *your* choice. It's mine, too. If the relationship doesn't work out, then it doesn't. I take my own risks, and I can handle my own lumps."

"Shortie?"

"*What?*"

"I love that temper you don't have. But we're not going to make love until you're ready," he said gently. "And that's that."

Seven

Men! Priss's paring knife flew. The bowl to her left was heaped with strawberries, the bowl to her right with the husks. Some husks and berries had escaped the bowls and littered the floor, counter and sink. The juice had already sneaked onto everything, including her hands, knees, chin and shorts. Making strawberry jam was a sticky, sticky, sticky process. Almost as sticky as understanding men.

Rinsing her hands for the dozenth time, she glanced at the recipe hung up by a clothespin. Sugar was next. And for ten quarts of strawberry jam, she needed mounds of it.

Naturally her spare sugar was at the very back of the bottom cupboard, where she had to burrow on her hands and knees to get it. Scowling, Priss thumped the five-pound container on the counter. She hadn't slept in two nights. Hadn't been hungry in two days. Her mood was as friendly as a pit bull's. That morning, Matt had asked her if she was coming down with the flu.

She wasn't coming down with the flu. The only thing wrong with her was being in love with the man next door.

And she couldn't remember, in her entire life, feeling this confused.

She'd never blatantly thrown herself at a man. Only Coop. The blasted man made a habit out of making things seem natural and right that had never been natural for her before. And on that raft, everything had seemed right. The way he looked at her, the way he touched, the emotions spiraling between them out of control. The terrible, vulnerable fear that she couldn't possibly satisfy a physical, lusty man like Cooper...Priss knew she'd been worried about it, but that fear just seemed to melt away on the raft. Desire had been a rage in her blood. Desire for *him*. Desire such as she never even knew existed. Desire he'd made her feel and then he'd quit. Just like that. With some patronizingly male chauvinistic comment about her not being ready.

Crossly Priss dumped in the first cup of sugar and started stirring. Ready? She'd been ready enough to climb walls. Did he think she didn't know her own mind? Did he think her incapable of knowing what she wanted, what she felt, what she needed? He'd treated her like a vulnerable virgin. He'd treated her like she needed some special kind of protection, as if he somehow suspected she'd been hurt sometime.

Bullcracky.

Yes, she'd been hurt once upon a time. But Cooper couldn't possibly know it. He'd never know it. And she couldn't conceivably have such powerful sexual feelings for him or behave as shamelessly wanton as she had if the past were any kind of problem. It wasn't.

Then why are you scared to see him again, Priss? Why have you avoided him for the past few days?

She hadn't avoided him. She'd been busy, doing the things she never had time for during the school year. Cleaning closets, painting shutters, making jam. She wasn't afraid to see him again.

She just wasn't absolutely positive how to handle Coop the next time he caught up with her. And one of these days—even as fast as she'd been moving—he was bound to catch up with her.

"Mrs. Neilson?"

Priss spun around in surprise, trailing sugar in her wake. Shannon's face was pressed against the screen door. "Come in, honey. Although I have to tell you that Matt's working."

"I know. I didn't come to see Matt. I came to see you." Shannon stepped in and glanced at the strawberry-sticky war zone. "I can see you're busy. But maybe I could help you?"

"Sure," Priss said, but she took one look at the girl's face and forgot the jam. Her heart squeezed tight. Shannon's hands were trembling; her skin was whiter than chalk, and globs of mascara were smudged under her eyes. "What's wrong?"

"Nothing," Shannon said, and promptly burst into tears. Not little tears, but huge, wrenching, gulping sobs.

Priss jammed the measuring cup onto the counter and sprinted across the room. Shannon was dressed in a spotless white shirt and shorts, but that couldn't be helped. Priss wrapped her sticky arms around her and started patting and soothing. "It's okay, it's okay. Nothing can be that bad. Try to tell me what's wrong, all right? Just try. Something must have happened . . ."

A violent nod. Then Shannon's head dropped right back on Priss's shoulder. "Last night . . . we had a fight. Me and Matt. And he's really, really mad at me."

Tomorrow Priss figured she'd be grateful that the problem was less serious than a nuclear holocaust. Just then, all she could think was that her son was definitely not going to appreciate his mother playing go-between. Unfortunately she didn't seem to have any other immediate choices. With one arm still clutched around Shannon, she reached for the Kleenex box by the phone. "It must have been pretty bad. Can you tell me what the fight was about?"

"No. I can't tell anyone. I'd die first." Shannon plucked a tissue and blew. Her eyes promptly welled up again.

"Okay."

"I really would die."

"Okay." Priss started mopping, that so pretty face, those so tragic eyes. The story Shannon couldn't tell tumbled out faster than a bubbling, blubbering brook. A couple of details were omitted in the wash, but Priss had no trouble figuring out that the pair had been fooling around last night. Necking. Probably more than necking.

"I thought he *liked* me. But he doesn't like me anymore. He thinks I'm cheap."

"My son said that to you?"

"He didn't say it. But that's what he thinks. Matt said…" Another rack of sobs cracked her voice. "He said he thought I'd kissed a lot of guys. And he didn't want to be just another guy on a long list. And Mrs. Neilson, I have…" Priss dabbed at the waterworks with another set of tissues. "I have kissed a lot of guys, but that was all. I mean, I told Matt that I'd done more than that. But I never did. I wanted him to think I was sophisticated, you know? I wanted him to think I was cool."

"Oh, honey." The years peeled back, as if exposing the raw skin of an onion. Priss remembered, painfully well, wanting a certain boy to think she was sophisticated and cool. And the devastating trouble she'd gotten into because of it. Guilt clawed through her conscience. She'd promised Coop that she would talk to Shannon. She'd meant the promise, but she'd been waiting for the right time. It felt like a strip torn off her heart, that she'd waited too long.

"What am I going to do?" Shannon wailed. "He hates me."

"No one hates you, honey."

"Well, he thinks I've slept around and that's almost worse. I can never face him again for as long as I live. I'm going to have to hide in the house for the rest of the summer. And how can I explain that to my dad?"

Priss put the kettle on and pulled up two kitchen chairs. By the time she served peppermint tea, they were past the dramatics and almost past the tears. It helped when the snow-white kitten climbed up on Shannon's lap. It also helped, Priss thought, that she'd been through this all before. In school, she had a sixth sense for the girls vulnerable to a certain kind of trouble.

"What you want to do about Matt, I don't know. In your shoes, I think I'd own up, tell him that you lied about some things because you wanted him to like you. I think he'd understand, but that's your decision, Shannon. Right now I want to talk about *you*, not my son. You got yourself in a situation that you didn't want. Let's talk about why that happened and how you can make sure it never happens again."

The soupy strawberry mixture congealed on the counter. The sun beat in hot by midafternoon. Priss didn't lecture. No teenager listened to a lecture. She talked about appearances, and how Shannon dressed and acted affected how other people saw her. She walked around the kitchen, role-playing, acting out femme fatales and shy mouses and bullies, making Shannon laugh, but trying to show her how body language sent out definite messages to other people. She talked about how people could get mistaken impressions, and she talked about rights. Shannon's right to say no. Her right to escape from any situation she wasn't comfortable with. Her right to not compound a lie or a mistake into thinking she was obligated, ever, to do anything she didn't want to do.

They veered way off the subject of the kids' spat, but Shannon didn't seem to notice. She liked the role-playing, liked talking about her values and the things that were important to her. By the time she ambled home, Priss felt both drained and satisfied. It was a tough world out there, especially for a young girl. But she'd managed to make Shannon think about some things without outright scaring her.

Then, of course, she glanced at the disastrous mess in her kitchen and winced. Possibly she could do without ten quarts of strawberry jam next winter.

What she couldn't do, unfortunately, was avoid Coop any longer. Priss eyed the telephone with the same affection she would show a rattler. If Cooper's daughter was going to live next door in any kind of harmony with her son, the two needed to have a little private time to chat. His Shannon might not want to talk to her Matt, but the opportunity could at least be created. If their respective parents were out for the evening.

Which meant that she had to call Coop.

When Cooper picked her up, it was past seven. His pants had a crease and his loafers were buffed. He was freshly shaved, freshly showered, freshly combed and on his best behavior.

Priss had made crystal clear that the sole purpose of this outing was to give the kids some time alone. She said she'd explain when she saw him. Cooper didn't need any explanations to know that he'd screwed up with Priss. Royally.

On the raft, days before, he'd been positive he'd done the right thing in calling a halt to their lovemaking. It was too soon. Priss had been extremely unsure of him in the beginning. Until he better understood her doubts and fears, he didn't want to push her. He didn't want her hurt. To pull back before they'd crossed the line to intimate sexual involvement . . . hell, isn't that what a gentleman should have done?

But for the past few days, she'd been playing zig to his zag. When he drove in, she was driving out. When he had free time, she was busy. When he called, she was in the shower.

And now, as she climbed into the plush seat of the Lincoln, she said, "Hi, Coop" in a voice as crisp as an alpine breeze. She hadn't given him that nobody-messes-with-me-buster look since the first day he was back in town.

The evidence was as clear as a cut-and-dried murder case.

He should never have been a gentleman.

God knew, he didn't want to make that mistake again, but he felt like a bungling elephant trying to tiptoe. Had he been that wrong in believing she needed more time? And how did a man go about getting himself out of such sticky, touchy feminine hot waters? Very carefully, he cleared his throat. "You look terrific, Shortie."

A pitiful understatement, but he could hardly risk mentioning that she looked on-the-spot ravishable. She'd used some feminine war paint, nothing excessive, but he rarely saw her in makeup at all. She'd done something to make those huge brown eyes look darker, deeper, sexier, and there was a slash of color on her lips. Her clothes weren't fancy—they were headed for the Stopaway, where no one dressed up—but her raspberry silk shirt and white jeans snuggled close to her trim curves. She looked like the niche in his heart that had been missing. She looked like the one woman, the only woman, he'd ever been terrified of losing.

"Thank you," she responded to the compliment, but the way he looked at her seemed to make her nervous. She fussed with her blouse collar, pulled on an earring and promptly switched subjects. "The reason I thought we should get away for a couple of hours—''

"I know. The kids had an argument. If we're out of the way, they'll have a better chance to patch it up."

"You already knew?" Priss asked in surprise.

"More or less. This morning I was finishing the deck off my bedroom, and ran out of sandpaper, so I stopped in the hardware store. Your son cornered me. He did a lot of foot shuffling and coughing, but apparently he was really upset that he'd hurt Shannon's feelings." He shook his head. "I have to admit, it felt off-the-wall weird trying to talk man-to-man with your son about my daughter."

There. Finally a real smile. "I know. It felt just as weird trying to talk woman-to-woman with your daughter about my son."

She warmed up once the conversation focused on the kids. She clearly appreciated all the time he'd spent with Matt. "I know he misses having a man around. It's not like I've ever avoided any subjects around him. But when we get into things like AIDS, drugs, sexual responsibility, I know I sometimes make him embarrassed. It's not just that I'm his mom, but that I'm female."

Coop had noticed. He also noticed that she easily and frankly talked about land-mine issues like sexuality. When it had to do with the kids, not them. "I didn't tell you what their argument was about."

"I assumed that you swore, cross your heart and hope to die, not to tell me," Priss murmured wryly.

Cooper chuckled as he turned into the parking lot for the Stopaway. "I did."

"So did I—swore on a pain-of-death vow—not to tell you. Isn't it fun, having teenagers?" She added seriously, "Coop? I like the connection I have with your daughter. I think she does, too. But I would never keep anything from you, if I thought Shannon was in real trouble."

"I know that, Shortie. The same way I'd tell you about Matt."

He angled into a parking slot and turned off the car. She reached down for her purse at the same time that he shoved his sunglasses onto the visor. For a second, accidentally, her palm brushed his thigh. Immediately her eyes bolted to his.

There was no flash of fire in the sun-dusty car. It just felt that way. Coop knew Priss trusted him with her son, and thought by now she knew she could trust *him*. But that rip-cord pull of desire between them always seemed to take her by surprise. In that instant, she looked as young as spring. A thousand times more fragile, more crushable, than the first bud on a tea rose. He could have kissed her in that instant. God knew, the way she suddenly licked her dry lips, the way she looked at him with those melted-chocolate soft eyes, was the same as an invitation.

But he'd seen that millisecond flash of wariness in her eyes. And he thought, *that's it. Damn you, Shortie, you're confusing the hell out of me and I'm scared of hurting you, and we're going to slow this down and that's that.*

"We'd better go in," he said gruffly.

"Sure," she said, but she glanced at the gravel parking lot as if noticing it for the first time. Her mind had been on him.

He scooted her inside fast, before he could be tempted again to take that kiss she'd been offering. If there was one place on earth guaranteed to cool his

overcharged hormones, it was the Stopaway. The
crowd inside rivaled the Atlanta freeways at rush hour.
There just were no other places to go for entertain-
ment in Bayville. With a hand at Priss's back, he
guided her past the restaurant section, since they'd
both already eaten dinner, and through a second pine-
paneled room that had a pool table, big screen TV and
bar.

The third room, in the back, had live music on
Thursday and Saturday nights, usually guitar and
banjo country fare. Babe O'Connell ran the place. The
walls were covered with an unlikely mix of local art
and antiques; tables were crammed in helter-skelter;
red leather booths lined the walls. Nothing matched.
No one cared. A harried waitress served them two
mugs of frosty beer and a bowl of peanuts almost before Cooper had seated Priss in the last booth left, a
far distance from the postage-size dance floor.

As he expected, everyone in the place knew Priss. A
half dozen people, all ages, stopped to chat before
she'd scooped up the first handful of peanuts. Apparently she was involved in everything from PTA to
the church to 4-H to any program in town that involved kids. The Bayville Summer Fair was coming
up; she was active in that, too. Someone had conned
her into manning a booth at the fair—a dunking
booth, he learned. He raised his eyebrows.

"Don't you say anything," she warned him. "All
the kids like to dunk a teacher, and nobody else would
volunteer. And the proceeds go for band uniforms.
How could I say no?"

For a kids' cause, Cooper thought, she was incapable of saying no. But that didn't mean he couldn't

tease her. "I'll help the cause. I'm a heck of a good shot."

"You buy one ticket, you die." Her threat was cut off when another couple stopped to chat. When they moved on, Priss rolled her eyes in a comical expression. "I should have stopped to think before we came here. I'm afraid the gossip tongues are going to wag, Coop."

He figured they would, too. It was the first time they'd been seen together in public. He liked the way people checked him over, then subtly glanced at Priss. He felt like a caveman, establishing his claim, announcing his ownership and protection—a concept that Priss would probably have leveled him for, but she didn't have to know.

Others ambled by—some to see him, remembering his dad, making a point of welcoming him back to town. Finally, for a short three-minute stretch, they were alone. Priss was having a good time, he thought. Until she snagged his wrist and jerked her head to the left. He looked.

On the far side of the room, a cowboy with a fringed shirt and a guitar was singing a Willie Nelson ballad about all the women Willie had loved. The dance floor was crowded.

Cooper shook his head in alarm. "I haven't danced in fifteen years, Shortie. That's the truth."

"We'll manage."

"I don't think so. In case you've forgotten, I'm a head taller than you. Dancing would be an acrobatic impossibility."

"We'll manage."

He tried again. "Have you seen the size of my feet? If I step on you even once, I'll probably break all your toes. You'll end up in the emergency room—''

Priss chuckled, but she was already angling out of the booth. Still snagging his wrist, she towed him behind her to the minuscule dance floor and promptly turned around and raised her arms.

He saw her face. Their heights were as disparate as a shrimp and a shark, and she'd started the evening, Coop knew, determined to keep an impersonal distance. But the liquid shine in her eyes was impossible to miss. A love of dancing was clearly Priss's Waterloo. And her total downfall—he should have guessed—was a lonesome, hopelessly sentimental ballad.

Without a qualm, she wrapped her hands around his neck. He thought, oh hell, and lowered his head. They had to look pretty silly, which didn't bother him. He was too worried about killing her if he stepped on her feet. There was only one place he'd ever had rhythm and it wasn't on a dance floor.

He snuggled the top of her head under his chin. The cowboy crooned on. The rest of the crowd blurred in his vision. His unavoidable klutziness on a dance floor didn't happen. Not with her. She molded so close he could feel the throb of her breasts, the warmth of her body. She fit him, in a way that had nothing to do with height or size. Desire swayed through his pulse, in unison with the swaying, humming rhythm of the love song. She had a body made for love songs. A body made for him.

Before the cowboy strung out the last chord, Coop managed to maneuver close enough to slip the singer a couple of twenties. "One more time," he said.

"You want the same song?"

The guitarist looked at him as if he were crazy. An accurate perception, Coop thought. Dancing with Priss was an exercise in torture that no sane man would ask for, and he hadn't changed his mind about going slow with her. Something was wrong. Something made her wary of him at a primitive, instinctive level. Until he knew exactly what it was, Coop knew damn well it was wrong to press for a deeper emotional relationship.

But she liked this song. And the whole damn world turned right for him when she was this close. He'd be good. He'd get tough with himself and exert total control over his emotions the rest of the night. But he just wanted a few more minutes with her laid against him like two sheets on a bed, with her hair under his cheek, tickling him, with her hands twined around his neck and that sleepy reckless look in her eyes when she tipped her head and looked at him.

"You told me you couldn't dance," she whispered.

"Maybe I needed the right teacher."

"I think it's pretty doubtful, Maitland, that you need a teacher for anything."

He feigned his most innocent expression. "Are you kidding? I don't know anything. I've been cloistered in the business world for years. I'm Mr. Conservative. In fact, there's probably no limit to what you could teach a shy, inhibited guy like me. Hey, you think that's funny, Shortie?"

She did, although there was a disarming flush on her cheeks when the dance finally ended. The music crew took a break. He led her back to the booth, thinking it was a damn good thing the place was even more crowded than before. Right then he wanted to be alone

with Priss. Completely alone. And his sense of honor
wasn't half as strong as that desire.

She'd barely touched her beer before, but she was
thirsty now. So was he. As he lifted the mug, he saw a
couple aiming toward them. He recognized the man,
but for a minute couldn't place him. Then it came.
Bric Eastman.

Bric and Cooper had both played football in high
school. Even in an oversized football crowd of play-
ers, the two of them had towered over everyone else.
Some said they looked alike, although Cooper could
never see it. Bric's hair was as blond as wheat, cut
short and Ivy League, and the only thing they'd ever
had in common was a walloping pair of shoulders.

They'd never been friends. All the Eastmans had a
tradition of seeking friends from a moneyed crowd.
Cooper never had time for that kind of snobbish nonsense, but it struck his dry sense of humor that Bric's
greeting was hearty and effusive. Apparently he was
worth a huge-time-of-day now that he had money
himself.

"Cooper?" The other man's hand shot out. "I
knew you were back in town. Don't know how we've
failed to connect before this. And this is my wife, Janet."

Cooper returned the handshake, then smiled for the
pretty, shy blond at Bric's side. Bric beamed a high-
voltage charmer of a smile on Priss. "And how are
you, Priss? Haven't seen you in a while."

"No complaints," Priss said crisply, and promptly
turned to his wife. "Congratulations, Janet, I heard
you were expecting."

Cooper's head whipped around. The two women
wiled away a few minutes talking pregnancies and

children. Their whole exchange was natural, easy, pleasant. Cooper had no idea what triggered the sudden, strong, disorienting sensation that something was wrong. Certainly there was no sign of stress in Priss's face.

In fact, for the first time since he'd known her, her face showed no expression at all.

He answered a question Bric asked him, but his gaze honed back like a laser beam on the pixie across the table. Priss responded instinctively and emotionally to everything—kids, kittens, stormy nights and love songs. When she was irked with you, you knew it. When she smiled, she smiled from the heart. When she was afraid or angry, or full of passion—God, especially when she was full of passion—she showed exactly what she was feeling in those big, dark eyes.

At the moment her smile was a prop. Her cheerful patter to the other woman a mindless dialogue. And how could no one else notice it? There was nothing. Nothing at all, in those big brown eyes.

Cooper looked at Bric again, at the other man's towering height, overwhelming size and felt something punch him, hard in the gut.

Clues pyramided on top of each in a rattled heap in his head. Priss's strange nervousness around him, when she handled every other man, woman and child with natural ease. His first and pervasive hunch that some man must have hurt or intimidated her sometime. His assumption that it must have been her husband, partly because he'd never fathomed why she'd picked out such an unlikely mate as David Neilson to begin with. It had never occurred to him that there might have been another man in her life before David.

He didn't like any of the conclusions that his mind was leaping to. He just couldn't seem to stop them. Every piece fit perfectly in the puzzle. He wished it didn't. All evening he'd carefully, tightly, put a leash of control on his emotions. It had seemed so important that he go slow with Priss. But that was before he'd envisioned a manipulative bastard like Bric hurting her. Maybe more than hurting her.

He told himself to take it easy. He didn't really know anything. Maybe he was making mountains out of molehills. Maybe he was imagining a bastard where none existed.

But he didn't think so. And when Bric smiled again, deliberately at Priss, charmingly at Priss, and said, "I understand we're both on the Bayville Summer Fair committee—"

Cooper slammed a hand on the table. Loud enough to swivel three pairs of startled eyes in his direction. "Sorry to cut this short, but I didn't realize the time," he said swiftly. "We both have teenagers expecting us at home, don't we, Priss?"

Priss opened her mouth to respond, but he didn't give her a chance to object. He yanked on her hand, hard enough to propel her out of that booth. And then he got her out of there.

Eight

When Cooper grabbed her hand, Priss didn't argue. Neither of their teenagers needed them at home, but she didn't say a word about that trumped-up excuse. Whatever Bric and Janet thought of their abrupt leave-taking, she didn't care.

He'd taken ill, she thought. And it happened so fast. As sudden as a summer storm, his face suffused with color. His shoulders had bunched up, every muscle rigid, and his eyes had the glitter-hard sheen of ice. He shuttled her through the crowd at the Stopaway, never releasing his manacle hold on her wrist until he'd pushed through the door and they were outside in the parking lot.

Instantly the confusion and bright lights of the restaurant disappeared. The night was a cool, quiet, dusty black. A single yard light pooled a circle of yellow in the gravel parking lot. Priss snagged his sleeve, determined to catch a clearer look at him, then worried when she did. His face looked chiseled in stone, and there was still a shock-dark brightness in his eyes. "You don't feel well," she told him.

The comment seemed to take him back. "I'm fine," he said shortly.

He was fine, like horses played hopscotch. Priss searched his face, trying to fathom what was wrong. Nothing happened in the restaurant that should have upset him. If anything, she'd been the one stressed by the steady barrage of people—at least certain people—but she'd been handling that kind of difficult situation for so many years that it was second nature. And that had nothing to do with Coop. "Is your stomach upset? Too many peanuts?"

"My stomach is fine."

"The crowd was packed in there. I tend to get claustrophobic, too, when there's too much noise and no room to breathe—"

"It wasn't that, either."

"What then?"

He opened his mouth, but then seemed to wrestle with what to say. He lifted a hand, then didn't seem to know what to do with it. Finally he said, "I'd like to talk to you, Priss. But not here, not near a crowd. And not near the kids. Let's go home, make sure our mutual offspring survived their evening, then clear the decks so we can have some uninterrupted time."

"All right." It never occurred to her to say no. He still looked like an avalanche of a problem was crushing his mind. If he needed her, she wanted to be there for him.

He dug into his back pocket and came up with the car keys. "Would you mind driving home?"

Her eyebrows zoomed halfway up her brow. "You want *me* to drive?"

It seemed he did. She plucked the keys and stole another look at his face, worrying now that the man was near death. Coop liked to be in control. She couldn't imagine him letting anyone behind the wheel unless someone was holding a gun to his head or he was imminently close to collapse. And it wasn't that she minded driving, but his Lincoln was a teensy bit different than her practical, no-frills Saturn.

She slid in, and discovered that her feet were six inches from reaching the pedals. She found the slot for the key, but there were a thousand confounded dials on the dash. She had to adjust the seat, the mirrors, find the lights. Temporarily she confused the thing for the wipers with the thing for the lights, and a splash of water pulsed on the windshield. "Now, don't you worry about a thing. I can handle this," she said firmly.

"I'm not worried. I know you can."

She appreciated his vote of confidence, but it wasn't deserved. Her Saturn was peppy, but when she put his Lincoln in reverse, the car shot back like a rocket. The brakes, thankfully, were just as responsive. Cooper never mentioned the sudden jolt, which rattled her even more. No man—in his normal mind—could resist climbing all over a woman for faults in her driving.

If he wasn't ill, he clearly wasn't in his right mind. Rapidly she pushed down the electric windows, thinking that the fresh air might make him feel better. To get him home safely, she simply had to concentrate on her driving. The car zoomed through the night like a jet. She barely touched the accelerator and the speedometer was on eighty. Carefully she slowed down. Still, the wind whipped through the windows in a gale of a draft, tossing her hair every which way and making her blouse collar flap like a boat sail.

Cooper had taken fifteen minutes to drive to the Stopaway. She pulled into his yard in eight minutes flat. After dousing the lights, she yanked the car keys from the slot and twisted around to hand them to him. Then she went still.

It was dark, but even in the velvet shadows, she could see his face. Prepared to defend any and all comments about her driving, Priss realized abruptly that she wouldn't need to. He hadn't noticed. He didn't care. His eyes were resting on her face, as if he'd been studying her the whole drive, absorbed, intent, as if some huge, heavy decision could be settled by the look of her.

"Coop," she said gently, "you're acting very, very weird."

"I know, Shortie. And I'm sorry. There was just something I had to think out." He pocketed the keys. "Now I have."

"And?" Surely he didn't think she would be satisfied with that vague explanation.

"And if you're not too tired, I still want some time with you."

"I'm not tired." There wasn't a prayer of her sleeping without knowing what was on his mind. Truthfully she didn't plan to budge until he started talking, but Cooper shook his head.

"You're going to worry about the kids until you know how their evening went. I'll check on Shannon. You check on Matt. If they're both settled and asleep, I'll meet you back outside in a few minutes."

Priss found the house quiet and Cleopatra waiting for her at the back door. Matt had left the lights burning, but he'd gone to bed. She peeked in his room and discovered him sprawled on his stomach, his rumpled head on the pillow, out for the count. Carrying Cleo, she explored the rest of the house, searching for clues...the kind of clues that no teen ever, ever seemed to realize that a mother could read like a road map.

Two glasses sat on the kitchen sink, one with lip gloss on the rim. Near the door was an empty two-liter bottle of soda. In the den, two throw pillows had been tossed on the carpet, one perched against a chair, the other against the couch... not together.

So, Priss thought. Shannon had come over. And they'd talked long enough to level that two-liter bottle of pop. And judging from the distance between the couch pillows they'd been talking, not necking.

Priss let Cleopatra down, and released a long, edgy sigh.

Cooper had been right. She would have worried all night if she hadn't come in and checked and discovered at least some evidence that Matt and Coop's daughter had survived their quarrel, that they hadn't forayed into deeper, murkier sexual waters, and for now were okay.

The kids were fine. It was Cooper who wasn't.

She'd never seen anything throw him before. He wasn't a man who was easily shaken, but something had obviously shaken him tonight. She'd imagined him in a temper before, had always expected that he'd blow with a lot of sound and fury but never that he'd go quiet. Coop just wasn't a quiet man. And she still had no idea what put that strange, sharp, shocked look of rage in his eyes.

A shiver feathered down her spine. If it were any other man, Priss would never have agreed to meet him. Not alone. Not isolated in the dark. By the time they drove home, he'd banked that anger, but she knew better than to invite a confrontation with a loose cannon. As a teenager there hadn't been an ounce of caution in her character; now it was as inbred and automatic as an instinct.

That she was willing to meet Coop underlined something she'd been afraid to say aloud. Even to herself.

She was in love with him. Deeply, seriously, dangerously in love. That wasn't news. But that she trusted him—*really* trusted him—came as a surprise. Coop might rant and rave in a temper, but she had absolutely no fear that he would ever physically hurt her.

She'd never given that kind of trust before.

She hadn't known she was capable of giving it.

And she suddenly felt the familiar sensation of sinking in quicksand. All these years she'd fiercely, stubbornly refused to believe that the jerk had affected her life. But he had. She'd loved and nurtured and taken care of other people, but there was a level where she'd always been alone. She'd never let anyone—even David—close enough to really hurt her.

Until Coop.

She swallowed hard. And then headed outside.

"And see? There's Orion."

"Cooper. That isn't Orion."

"No? Well, did you see that one up there? Hepa-cutrux. There's a long complicated legend about that star—"

"I've never heard of a star by the name of Hepa-cutrux."

"Maybe we should stick with the familiar. Like that one. The Little Dipper. See it?"

"Coop?"

"Hmm?"

"The Little Dipper is on the other side of the sky. What you know about stars wouldn't fit a thimble, Maitland." Priss rolled over on her side and perched on an elbow. "And you didn't bring me out here to stargaze."

"True," Cooper admitted. "But I wanted to hear you laugh. And you have been. In fact, I have another idea..."

Priss wasn't sure she was ready for "another idea." Bemused, she watched Cooper leap to his feet and stride for the car.

When Coop picked her up, she'd expected to hear a serious and weighty discussion. So far, she hadn't heard anything come out of his mouth that wasn't kissing kin to nonsense. He'd driven them to the field of red clover by the pond—a logical enough location for a quiet, uninterrupted conversation.

But then he'd brought out a bottle of wine, two glasses, a corkscrew, a wedge of cheese and some crackers because "no one could have a serious conversation without something to munch on." Then he'd unfurled an old woolen army blanket because "we can't eat standing up and it's damp on the ground." Then had come his shy, modest claim that he was an expert at identifying the star constellations. More hooey.

Now, Priss watched in disbelief as he leaned in the driver's door of the Lincoln. She heard the sounds of squeaky static. Then two seconds of a weather report. Then the ancient strains of Bill Haley urging the world to shake, rattle and roll. Cooper left the radio channel there, closed the car door and aimed back for her with an unholy grin.

"Would you like to dance, Ms. Neilson?"

"The only thing I want to do is take your temperature. There's clearly something wrong with you. In case you haven't noticed, we're in the middle of a field in the middle of the night—"

"Come on." He cupped his hand and motioned her up. "You know you love to dance. And I shuffled you out of the Stopaway so fast that we didn't have another chance."

She tried again. "This song is older than the hills. And I think it's a jitterbug. Do you have any idea how to do a jitterbug?"

"None," he admitted and tugged her to her feet. "You'll have to show me."

Priss didn't want to let him get away with it. Whatever had upset him at the Stopaway...she wanted to know, wanted to help him if he'd let her. But Cooper, truly, no longer showed a trace of that strange, dark mood. And she could understand, better than anyone, that sometimes you couldn't talk. Sometimes it only hurt to talk, and the best thing you could do for someone else was simply be there.

Coop wanted her with him. She had no doubt about that.

And he wanted, right now, to play. He made that just as clear.

So she showed him, the toe-heel, toe-heel, swing back of the jitterbug. She showed him how to shimmy. She showed him how to twist. The big lummox had two left feet. It didn't help that their dance floor was a dew-soaked clover field, lit only by a wisp of a moon. Priss kept expecting little men bearing straight jackets to find them and take them away to the funny farm.

But no one found them. And Coop's big, roisterous laugh made her laugh with him, and twisted something soft in her heart. He was having fun. In spite of his extensive, vast and violent claims about being lazy, he barely knew how to relax. For him to let down his hair and really do something mindless and silly...he was doing it now, with her, and she loved it.

The car stereo volunteered oldie after oldie. "Johnny Be Good." "Rock Around The Clock." "Blue Suede Shoes." He *loved* "Blue Suede Shoes." And then the announcer chose another song, another oldie, a slow, lonesome tune about a boy asking his girl if she wanted to dance under the moonlight.

Cooper held out his arms. She moved in, as naturally as a homing pigeon for its nest. He didn't have two left feet when the rhythm was slow. His body was warm. So was hers. His heart was thundering. So was hers. She nestled her cheek in his chest, eyes closed, not looking at him but only aware. Aware of him.

Do you wannnnna dance....

The boy in the song sounded so young. She suddenly felt that vulnerably young. Young and wistful and yearning...and hopelessly in love with the man who held her in his arms. Her feet were soaked from the dew-drenched field. She didn't care. The meadow glistened like platinum under the pale silver moon. Stars cuddled in the folds of a black velvet sky. A sleepy owl *whooed* in the distance. She could smell the trees, the pond, the pungent fresh scent of clover. It was all magic.

But Coop was the real magic. When he lifted his head, she lifted hers. Though the love song had stopped playing, she could swear she still heard it. A slow, silky shiver started in the pit of her belly when she saw the look in Cooper's eyes. Still swaying, still in motion, he reached for the top button of her blouse. Then the second button.

When the blouse gaped open, he pulled it free from her jeans. Slower than slow motion, slower than time, his big warm hands slid the fabric off her shoulders. The blouse drifted to the ground. She didn't watch him pull off his own shirt; she couldn't tear her eyes away from his face. But then his shirt was gone, too. He flicked the catch of her bra. Her breasts were suddenly, painfully exposed to the moonlight. And then they weren't, because he pulled her close again.

They danced. She didn't know how long. The radio announcers changed at midnight. The new one played sleepy jazz. It didn't matter what he played; Cooper moved to his own rhythm. It was a rhythm she knew. A rhythm and beat that her whole body knew. His jeans glued to her jeans. His arousal rubbed against her lower abdomen, hot, hard, wanting. Her bare breasts, her soft skin, throbbed to the sensation of his naked chest. He didn't kiss her. He did nothing to indicate this wasn't all he wanted—to indulge in a little dirty dancing, half bare but not all bare, under the moonlight and a star-dusted sky.

Her whole heart had gone quiet.

It wasn't all he wanted. His eyes had turned deep and dark and liquid black. He'd looked at her that way before. Then hurt and completely confused her by claiming that she wasn't ready. She didn't know then, didn't know now, what he'd meant. She only understood, in every intuitive nerve in her feminine body, that he'd changed his mind. He wanted to make love. Now. Tonight.

If she was willing.

Her hands were unsteady and slippery as they skidded down his chest. Brazenly—God, she'd never been so brazen—she unlatched his belt buckle, then tipped her head back to look at him. He towered over her like a redwood tree. Her heart started fluttering like a quaking aspen.

He watched her undo his belt, watched her stumble over the unfamiliar snap of his jeans. His gaze skimmed over her bare white shoulders, the shadowed swell of her breasts. He'd stopped smiling a long time ago. The skin was stretched taut over his cheekbones, the muscles tight in his jaw. His face had a harshness she'd never seen, a harshness that she could have, maybe should have, been afraid of. And in his eyes was a dare. An uncompromising, no-crying-uncle, masculine dare. The low rasp of his voice communicated the same dare. "What do you want, Priss?"

"You."

The single word echoed in the darkness, vibrated between them. Still, he made no move to touch her.

"Maybe I don't believe you. You were afraid before. Maybe you still are."

"No." It was a lie of love, she told herself. It wasn't his fault that she had fears. She never wanted the shadows in her life to touch him. Still, her word didn't so easily convince him.

"Prove it," he whispered. "Prove to me that this is what you want, love. Show me that you're not afraid."

She tugged his head down and kissed him the way he, so many times, had kissed her. No inhibitions, no hesitations, just an openmouthed seductive invitation to lose herself in the senses of touch and taste. He'd done it to her. Now, like a surprise, she discovered the heady feminine power of being able to do it to him.

He moved, midkiss. He moved both of them, by hooking his hands around her waist and simply lifting her. It was easier to kiss him when his mouth was at the same height as hers. He carried her to the rough woolen blanket. They both sank down. He severed the kiss long enough to shuck off her shoes, then his. Then he knelt, waiting.

It took her a floundering, dizzy minute to figure out what he was waiting for. Permission. "Jeans," she said.

"You want our jeans off?"

She found her voice. "I want ... everything off."

Still he waited. "Naked will change things. I think you need patience from me. I think you're counting on my control. I can't promise you either one, Priss. If you want a gentle, careful lover, I'm not your man. So you'd better be damn sure this is what you want."

That slow bourbon-and-whiskey dare was still in his voice. She was briefly tempted to hit him. She knew David would never have put her through this. A gentleman would have the courtesy to seduce her when she'd clearly asked to be seduced. A gentleman would have made it easier for her. A gentleman would have helped.

But Coop, she'd always known, was nothing like David. In the deepest intuitive sense, she understood that was why Coop scared her. And yet, conversely, why the pull for him was so strong. She didn't test tigers. Yet she wanted to test him. Recklessness had been drilled out of her character. Yet she felt reckless with him, reckless and even angry, for making her aware that she'd missed something—a depth of emotion, a depth of love—because she'd been scared. Pit-deep scared, all these years. Scared to let go. Scared to ever let anyone have power over her ever again.

Maybe it wasn't her who raised up and peeled off her jeans without another word. Maybe it wasn't her who as bare as the day she was born reached over and tugged at his. A roar filled her ears. She knew her fingers were trembling. The night had long turned cool, yet her whole body was suffering from fever, a heat she couldn't escape, a shivering fretfulness that she couldn't shake.

He was awesome naked. Bigger than in clothes, bigger than in life. All muscle and sinew, power and strength. And aroused. Lord, was he aroused. Her husband had been so nice and small and comfortable.

Coop was probably going to kill her, and damn him, if she didn't love him so much, she'd cut and run right now.

"Nothing's happened yet," Cooper whispered. "You can still call it off. But you'd better be quick. Because in about ten seconds from now, I'm afraid I just might spontaneously combust, Shortie."

She needed reassurance. Not another warning. She pushed him down, leveling him against the scratchy woolen blanket, and silenced him with a hard, hot kiss. She didn't want to hear any more warnings. They just made her scared. And if he was determined to make her feel desperately, terrifyingly vulnerable, she wasn't going to be alone. She was taking him down with her.

Coop could be made to feel vulnerable, too. Easily she discovered. It was amazingly easy to make him shake. Anything did it. The whisper brush of her hands on his chest. The swirl of her tongue in his mouth. The rub of her bare, soft thigh against the hair-roughened length of his.

She forgot to worry. He meant so much to her. She thirsted to show him, hungered to express how huge those feelings were. Pleasing him demanded all her concentration. Loving him, the way she wanted him to feel loved, became a consuming need. She nipped the curve of his shoulder, trailed teasing kisses down his abdomen, absorbed in him, thinking only of him. Yet his fierce responsiveness seemed to helplessly trigger her own. The scent and temperature of his skin, the feel of him, ignited a fire of desire in the hollow of her belly. The sound he made when his breathing roughened, tightened, hoarsened, made that fire lick hotter. But the best, the burn of real flame, came from the look in his eyes when he lost all control.

When he rolled her over, she expected, anticipated, his possession. And didn't get it. He hurt her, when his mouth nuzzled roughly at her breasts. It hurt good. His hands ran over her skin, arousing itchy, restless feelings like tiny forest fires. She felt hot where he touched, and there was no part of her that he didn't

touch. Coop didn't understand about inhibitions.
She'd known he wouldn't go slow. She'd known. But
he could have given her a minute to catch her breath.
He could at least have had the sensitivity to realize that
she was embarrassed when he discovered how wet she
was between her thighs, and he hurt her again when he
stroked. His fingers had turned gentle, tender, exqui-
sitely careful. He hurt her unbearably. She called his
name. The sound came out like a wild, rough whisper, half groan, half demand. She wanted him to cover
her. She wanted him inside her. Now.

Yet he didn't cover her. He stroked a hand down her
sleek damp skin and then laid back, pulling her on top
of him. She didn't understand. He framed her face in
his hands, kissed her again and again and again. Or
maybe she was kissing him. It was all the same by
then. Both of them were shaking. His skin was as salty
and sweaty-slick as hers. His heart was a primitive
drumbeat, matching her own. And everything she'd
ever been afraid of paled beneath the basic fear that
she was going to die if they didn't end this soon.

"Slow down, love," he murmured.

"No."

"I'm not going to take you, Priss."

If he thought he was leaving her in this shape, he
had another think coming.

"You're going to take me," he whispered.

It sunk in why he wanted her on top. The vague
thought filtered through her mind that the blanket was
scratchy and the ground hard beneath it and Coop was
trying to be considerate. But another, sharper perception followed that one. For all their wild love play,
he'd never pinned her, even playfully. He'd never
given her the chance to feel overpowered or threat-

ened by the differences in their physical size or
strength.

For wanting to protect her, she loved him, but that
cause was already lost. She'd never felt more overpowered, more overwhelmed. Her world splintered
into sensations—the feel of his hands on her hips,
guiding her over him, his rough, coaxing murmurs of
praise, his eyes calling her closer, closer, until she
obeyed his demanding plea for yet another kiss and by
that time he was easing inside her.

Her eyes misted. Not from hurt. He filled her up,
intimately, completely, but that physical sensation
fused with the release of pure emotion. Years swirled
away. She'd been joyful once. She'd anticipated be-
longing to a man, had blindly assumed that carnal love
was a natural extension of sharing heart and spirit.
She'd come across evil and survived it, but nothing
had been the same. A single night had destroyed that
kind of soft, fragile innocence.

He gave it back to her. That joy, that wonder. It was
plumb crazy to feel innocent, when the pagan devil
beneath her was wickedly, wickedly squeezing her behind and whispering disgraceful things. He told her to
take him. He told her to ride him, hard and unholy
fast. He told her to let go, just let go, just let go...

And she did, lifting her head, her white throat bare
to the silver satin moonlight. Freedom. Freedom came
from loving him. Her body moved for him, with him,
until pleasure spasmed through her like a healing burst
of light. Her heart soared higher than an eagle's. And
then Coop wrapped her up, and pulled her down into
his warm strong arms.

Nine

Holy Mackerel. Priss's eyes popped open on the star-dusted sky. She felt like a sail puffed up with wind. A rosebud busting open. A new butterfly climbing out of its cocoon for its first drink of sun.

She propped up on an elbow, ready to share some of that unquenchable exuberance. Unfortunately the only one she wanted to share it with was lying next to her, as worn-out as a tuckered hound.

A soft smile tugged the corners of her mouth. Coop's hair looked like a tornado wind had combed it. His forehead still showed traces of dampness. The only movement in his long, long body was the deep, steady rise and fall in his chest. The operative word was wasted.

She'd put him in this shape. *Her.* Who'd have guessed it? She'd been so sure that making love with him would be a test of performance and inadequacy.

By nature she was affectionate, but passion was so different. In her marriage, she'd studied her husband like a dead-serious student, learning what he liked, caring deeply that she not disappoint him. She'd desperately hoped that experience would help her please Cooper.

It hadn't. No experience, no technique, no previous knowledge had been worth a grain of rye with Coop. She stroked his neck, feeling a huge, consuming wave of love. He needed her. She'd never believed that before tonight. He'd come alive for her, apart for her, a strong sure man laying bare a vulnerable and lonely soul. If she'd been wild for him, it was his own fault. Loving him had been all she could think of, all she'd known how to do. But Lord, she'd never expected such cataclysmic results.

Priss assumed he was catnapping, but gradually realized that his eyes were open, warm and indulgent on hers. "You're worrying me with that smile, Shortie. If you're in the mood again I have to warn you that an old man needs a little recovery time."

"Poor baby. Advanced age catching up with you?"

Slowly his arm lifted, as if it were too exhausted to move fast. Just as slowly his hand arched in midair, hovered and then zoomed down to mercilessly tickle her ribs. She squirmed, laughing, then nestled close to the warmth of his side. In the hush of night, the air was cool and damp. But not next to him.

"Coop?"

"Hmm?"

She wanted to tell him that nothing would ever be the same. She wanted to tell him that her whole world had suddenly tipped in a new and fragile direction. But Coop had no way to understand where she'd been; the words would just sound corny. She stumbled for a way to express her feelings in a way he might believe. "I thought I knew...everything about making love. But it was never, ever, that special for me before."

"Special? I'd call it a lot closer to earth-shattering." He shifted on his side, his gaze treasuring her face, her eyes, her mouth. "You earth-shattered me, Ms. Neilson. Even worse than I expected. And believe me, I was expecting trouble—knowing you."

She had to smile. "Knowing *me?* What have I ever done to cause you trouble?"

"Everything. I was living in a nice, safe glass house until I came back home and found you. You made me laugh. You made me feel again. You make me *think,* Shortie. You've thrown me—literally as well as figuratively—and I was really worried about making love with you. You're such a sensualist. So full of natural emotion. I was afraid I wouldn't know what to do. I mean, for a conventional guy like me, with such limited sexual experience . . ."

Priss chuckled. She didn't believe a word—he was only trying to make her feel good, but heaven knew, it was working. She felt a million warm fuzzies from her head to her toes. "It's true," she said gravely, "that I have vast experience in making love."

"I figured that out. God, were you good . . ."

"But not as good as you."

He wouldn't let her win the argument, no matter how many valid points she raised. Somehow it was easy, making teasing, nonsense love talk with him. Easy to believe they'd been lovers forever even when Priss was suddenly, bewilderingly unsure how they'd ended up making love at all this night. Days ago, he'd pulled back as if a more intimate relationship was not what he wanted. Hours ago, he'd been disturbingly shaken by something at the Stopaway.

"Uh-oh. That cocky feminine smile disappeared," he murmured.

She smiled again, but it was a softer, quieter smile. "Are you ever going to tell me what was wrong earlier tonight?" When he didn't immediately respond, she touched his cheek. "I understand, if it's something you feel you can't talk about. I won't pry. I was just worried because you were obviously upset."

He hesitated, then angled his head to look straight in her face. He'd looked at her with that same disturbingly intent expression before. "You're right. I was. The problem . . . was seeing Bric Eastman at the Stopaway."

In the gash of a second, her whole body went still. A lump as sharp as a broken shard of glass filled her throat. She couldn't seem to escape Cooper's steady, quiet gaze. "Heavens," she said casually. "I knew you played football together. I assumed you two were old friends."

"We played football. We were never friends."

"You don't like him?"

"When we were kids, I thought he was an arrogant, spoiled, manipulative bastard. Nothing I've heard since I've come home has made me think the leopard changed its spots. Don't ever, ever, feel that you have to be nice to him because of me, Priss."

"Okay."

Gently, softly, he feathered back her hair. "You're not saying what you think of him. And suddenly it occurs to me . . . you've always had to be nice to him, haven't you, Shortie? It was the Eastmans who built your father's church. And they've always been big donors. Unless that's changed?''

"No. Especially in the years after my mom died, I don't think my dad could have survived without them. The farmers had several tough financial years in a row. The town just couldn't have supported the church . . . not without help from the Eastmans.''

"So your dad was financially dependent on the Eastmans," Cooper murmured. "One more puzzle piece that fits in place.''

"Puzzle piece? I don't understand." If she could stop her heart from hammering so hard, maybe she could think. She'd never made the association to Coop's sudden change of mood and Bric. There'd seemed no reason to. Over the years she'd had to see and talk to Bric a million times. To her knowledge she'd never shown in her face or voice or in any conceivable way that she felt less than neighborly toward the man. Only why, then, was Coop coming up with all these questions?

Yet that seemed the end of them. He was still stroking her hair, a touch as gentle as silk. Still looking at her with that strange, sharp concentration. Then suddenly, from nowhere, he bent down and kissed her. Hard.

When he got around to lifting his head, he surveyed her flushed face and distractedly sleepy eyes. His thumb traced the swell of her bottom lip. "Priss, I want you to know something. There is nothing you could tell me—*nothing*—that could change how I feel about you. Would you try to believe that?''

She tried to answer him. And instead felt herself shivering suddenly. A ghost wind trembled through the trees. A cluster of clouds covered the moon.

"You don't want to talk about deep, dark secrets tonight?" he murmured.

She shook her head.

"Earlier, you said you understood if I couldn't talk about something. That goes both ways, Priss. I know exactly how hard some things are to talk about. In fact, I think we're more alike than you know." He glanced up, then reached over his head to the spot where he'd thrown his shirt. He wrapped it protectively around her shoulders. "At different times in my life, when I was really in trouble, do you know who I turned to?"

"Who?"

"No one. I don't lean easily on other people. And I don't think you do, either."

"No," she admitted.

"I was raised, as a man, to depend on myself. To lead, not to follow. To take my knocks on the chin. To believe that laying my problems on someone else was a cardinal sin of weakness."

She easily responded. "I was raised, as a woman, to take care of other people. To believe that a good woman doesn't burden the people she loves. She's strong enough to cope no matter what happens. To do less would be selfish."

He nodded. "And then it gets worse once you've grown up, doesn't it? You find out that the people around you need your strength. They're used to it. They count on it. And when people are depending on you, how can you let them down?"

"Oh, Coop. I know. I understand exactly."

"I had a feeling you would. I had a feeling you were the one woman on the entire planet who would. I'm afraid it's your own damn fault I've fallen in love with you, Shortie."

Again her whole body went still but for an entirely different reason this time. She knew she was in love with him, and she knew he had strong, true feelings for her—friendship and desire and caring. Beyond that, she hadn't believed or let herself think about.

"I love you," he repeated. "Really. Love you. Did you think I was joking when I said I wanted all or nothing?"

Priss swallowed. "I may have thought...that you meant that in a sexual sense."

"No." His tone was low and emphatically clear. "No matter how strong the chemistry, I'd never have touched you if I thought that was all we had going for us. Maybe you don't believe that yet, but you will. You're not used to trusting anyone at that gut level. No one can understand that better than I do. But when you're ready to turn to me—if you'll just take that one risk, Priss—I'll be there for you."

And then he reached for her.

Crumbs spattered everywhere when Priss sliced the day-old crusty bread. She forked the slice, waded it through the nutmeg and egg yolk mixture, then lifted it to the sizzling griddle. French toast was Matt's favorite breakfast. She'd made it a zillion times. Never before, though, when she hadn't had a lick of sleep.

Coop hadn't brought her home until after 5:00 a.m. A predawn haze had already turned the sky a smoky gray. Farmers were already out in their fields. Roosters were crowing and the birds were up, and he'd laid her against her back screen door and kissed her as if he were a greedy glutton who was starving for a feast. But he had already feasted on her. Twice.

Priss lifted the edge of French toast. As black as tar. As ruined as the last three pieces she'd tried.

She forked the charred bread into the disposal, and drizzling egg yolk, flopped another piece of bread onto the skillet. Her son was going to be up any minute. She simply had to concentrate. Yet concentration was nearly impossible when her whole body still felt alive and aware and embarrassingly tender from Coop's prolonged lovemaking. He'd made it clear—unforgettably clear—that he wanted her to be part of his life. How was she supposed to think about breakfast?

"Morning, Mom."

She jumped before whirling around. Her son couldn't have any idea what she was doing in a clover field at five in the morning, but she'd die a guilty maternal death if he did. Soon, very soon, she needed to talk to Matt about Cooper. But not this morning. "Good morning, honey. Sleep well?"

"Just great." Matt wandered in, yawning, already dressed for work in jeans and a clean T-shirt. He took one look at the kitchen. "Holy kamoly. What happened?"

"Anyone can burn a couple pieces of toast," she said firmly.

"Yeah? Some days, Mom, you're not safe let loose in a kitchen." He stole the spatula from her hand with a grin.

Priss let him putter at the stove—her son wasn't a bad cook—while she placed silverware and plates on the table. By the time he carted over the platter of French toast, they'd talked about the weather, his work schedule, the price of "old man Harmon's" jalopy and Stuart Bell's new horse. Everything, Priss noted, but Shannon.

Matt was still making fast small talk when they both settled at the breakfast table. Eventually, though, he stopped chowing down long enough to clear his throat. "If you haven't already figured it out, Shannon was over here last night." He lifted his fork. "I know you don't like kids in the house when you're not here. But when she knocked on the door, I couldn't see leaving her on the porch. She was kind of upset."

"Oh?"

"Don't give me that 'oh,' Mom. She said she'd already talked to you. So, yeah, we had a fight. I said some stuff I shouldn't have. So did she." He added, "It's all over now. In fact, I'm probably going to take her to the fair."

"Okay." Priss hesitated, well aware that was all her son wanted to say. A parent who pried too hard could easily shut off communication instead of inviting it. Still, she couldn't quite let it go. "Matt...she's had a lot of changes going on in her life. I think that makes her particularly vulnerable to being hurt right now."

He shrugged. "She's mixed up, anyway. Blows hot and cold like a fan switch. But it's not like either one of us are looking for something heavy duty, you know? I'm not going to get any girl pregnant, mess up her life, mess up mine. And Shannon's okay. Nothing's going to happen to her when she's with me. Like I'll protect her, you know?"

"I think she could use a little protecting. I also think she's really lucky to have a friend like you. Have I told you recently that I'm glad you're my son and that I'm enormously proud of you?"

"For cripes sakes, Mom. You know I hate it when you say embarrassing stuff like that."

"Sorry. I try to remember, but sometimes things like that just sneak out. And speaking of sneaking out . . . did you happen to notice the time?"

"Yikes!" Matt glanced at the clock, shoveled in one more bite and then lurched out of his chair. "I'm gonna be late for work if I don't hustle, but I still have to tell you one more thing."

"What?"

He stopped at the door long enough to jam his feet into high tops, then stood up. She could hardly miss the mischievous grin. "If you're going out with Mr. Maitland again, we need to have a little talk about ground rules. Like I got up at two to get a glass of water and you weren't in yet. I turned on the porch light." He waggled his forefinger in a gesture she'd certainly seen before since she'd done it to him. "It's okay, since I knew you were with Mr. Maitland. But next time—house rules—you should leave me a note so I know where you are and that you're okay."

The coffee mug between her palms seemed to be suspended midair. "Yes, sir."

He grinned again. "It's a heck of a job, raising a mother. But hey, I'm up for it."

A moment later, he'd slammed the door. Priss thought, *You're getting awfully big for your britches, Matthew Neilson.* But she was smiling as she tackled the dishes. Her son might have a dreadfully tactless hand with the female of the species, but that could be attributed to youth and inexperience. His instincts were true. He'd always been protective of any creature smaller than himself—including her. More relevant, he had the good judgment to sense that Cooper's daughter needed someone to watch over her.

Shannon was her son's first exposure to a little female dynamite. Priss thought he was handling it well.

She only wished she were doing half so well at handling the dynamite package that was Shannon's father.

Her mind was functioning on automatic, blurry from lack of sleep. She needed rest before she could think about Cooper. But that proved worthless advice. Leaving the griddle to soak, she climbed the stairs to her bedroom. She pitched off her clothes, slid bare between the ice-blue sheets and closed her eyes.

Her eyes popped right back open again. The morning sun shone in, bright as life. If her mind was a spinning atom, Coop was definitely its nucleus.

As of last night, he was her lover. More than that, Priss poignantly knew, he was her first love. She hadn't understood the difference before, had never comprehended that as deeply as she'd loved David, she'd never been in love with her husband. She'd never been in love with anyone. At the time of life when most girls were discovering love, Bric Eastman had already happened in her life. One afternoon she'd been a girl. By morning she'd been old.

Her gaze focused blindly on the sunlight speckling the comforter. Coop claimed to love her. Really love her. He hadn't mentioned rings yet, but Priss suspected that was coming. Once Cooper knew what he wanted, he charged ahead with full speed and absolutely no patience. He'd want an answer.

In principle, Priss had that answer from the depth of her heart. She'd never been playing with him. The stakes, for her, had always been serious. She'd never find another man she loved like Coop, and in the rare moments when her confidence was high, she even believed she was good for him. Left alone, God knew what addlepated projects the man might get into. He needed some feminine steerage, someone to stand up to him, someone to temper that all-or-nothing temperament. He trusted her. They shared laughter, values, understanding, and heaven knew, passion. He was everything in a man that she'd once dreamed of.

Yet her heart was suddenly pounding, pounding, pounding.

She couldn't seem to forget all the questions he'd asked about Bric. More relevant, she couldn't forget Cooper's tone of voice when he'd asked her to take a risk and trust him. His tone had been quiet and compassionate and steeped in his special brand of gentleness. Coop knew she was keeping something from him. And he'd asked her to trust him.

But he couldn't specifically know about Bric, Priss told herself. For almost twenty years, she'd guarded that secret as carefully as antique glass. No one knew, except for the one man who would never admit what he'd done. Initially she'd responded to Coop's overwhelming size with fear—his only possible reason to suspect something had happened to her—but that was done. She knew Cooper now. The panic reaction no longer existed. What happened long ago was ugly and dirty; she might risk everything if she told him, and for what? That ancient history didn't matter anymore.

Or so she'd tried to convince herself for the past nineteen years.

Priss wearily rubbed her temples. Coop, damn him, had opened up so many emotional doors that she'd assumed were dead bolted. He made her feel things she

hadn't felt in years. The hot flame of desire. Trust.
The sweet need of a woman for a man, the even
sweeter joy of finding a man who needed her. Fragil-
ity, wonder, the challenge of discovering someone she
could grow with.

And part of loving him was the desire, the huge desire from her woman's heart, to be as unconditionally
honest with him as he'd been with her. Possibly, Priss
thought, that wasn't even a choice. She was frighten-
ingly certain that she'd never be able to keep secrets in
Cooper's bed. Or out of it.

What mattered, though, was that if she loved him
the right way she shouldn't want to.

With the eraser edge of a pencil, Cooper punched in
the local telephone number for Mrs. Jeffries. Over the
past two weeks, he'd either phoned or personally met
with three separate Iowa bankers, several board
members of the local farmer's co-op, a commodities
broker from Chicago and now—if his luck held—he
hoped to connect with the widow Jeffries.

That unlikely and eclectic group of contacts would
seem to have nothing in common. But there was a link.
Bric Eastman.

God, Cooper thought, it was fun to have money.

Whistling while he waited for the connection, he
lifted his long legs to the counter and lazily crossed his
ankles. His gaze wandered over the kitchen with satisfaction. A bay window and skylights definitely
brightened up the room. The work island, oak cupboards, paprika counters and new floor were all done.
The only project left to do was wallpaper, and Priss
and the kids had agreed to gather after lunch to tackle
that together.

He had ample time to handle some business first.

A querulous, quavery voice finally answered the phone. Cooper jammed the pencil behind his ear. "Mrs. Jeffries? This is Cooper Maitland, George's son. I know you knew my dad. He always spoke of you and Frank so highly... listen, I understand you own the right-of-way on the acreage off Chilsom Road. I heard you might be interested in selling it... no kidding?"

Fifteen minutes later, Coop hung up the phone. It wasn't a done deal—nothing was a done deal until money changed hands—but a verbal promise had been made. Damned if he knew what he was going to do with the right-of-way on Chilsom Road. Bric was the one who wanted it. Eastman could even still have it— but not for the price he'd tried to cheat the widow Jeffries out of.

The Jeffries deal was peanuts. Bayville, Coop had discovered, had been suffering hard times. A stubborn drought had seriously crippled many farmers. The recession had added to their woes. It was hardly surprising that one particular local landowner was overextended in such a precarious financial period. It was a no-no, however, for a grower to borrow money from the co-op to speculate in grains futures. And an even more serious no-no to get caught.

Eastman had a wife and four children. Cooper didn't prey on women and children. He had no intention of ruining Bric.

He just wanted to hurt him.

Priss's face spun in his mind. All he'd had to do was mention the bastard's name and her skin had turned whiter than alabaster. She hadn't told him what happened, not the first night they'd made love, not in any of the fourteen nights since then. He'd wanted her to. He'd needed her to take that leap of trust.

The last thing he wanted to do was cause her pain. God knew, he had no desire to force her into talking about something that hurt her. There'd be no need if Eastman wasn't still affecting her life.

The few private hours they'd managed to steal in the past two weeks, they'd made love. Incredible, searing, soul-binding love. By now, Priss probably thought that making love with her on top was his sexual preference. Coop had a million sexual preferences. All of which he wanted to try on her, to her, with her. But not if she panicked at the hint of his greater weight and size. And no matter how winsome and wild her response in bed, no matter how lovingly and naturally they cleaved out of bed, she got shook up and nervous when he even gently hinted at a future.

What had happened to her was somehow unfinished business. And Coop knew, from the rock-hard part of his gut, that he was going to lose her if she didn't settle it. Soon. She'd never tolerate an affair for long—not with two observant teenagers in house and a nosy town that watched their every move. But he was never going to get a ring on her finger unless she conquered her fear of commitment to him.

Coop clawed a hand through his hair. He'd never played for stakes like this before. He didn't know what the right thing to do for her was. His whole life, he'd gone after whatever he wanted like a blundering moose. Bluster and strength worked for him. But subtlety? Sensitivity? Hell. He felt like an elephant trying to tiptoe. And failing badly.

He glanced at the clock. It was nearly noon. The clan was scheduled to gather in another hour. He knew they'd have fun. The four of them always did. Shortie couldn't help but notice how terrifically they functioned as a family. Maybe, today, it would make a difference.

But he didn't believe that. What really mattered, at a heart level, was between him and her alone.

And Cooper couldn't shake the fear that he was fast, very fast, running out of time.

Ten

Damned if Cooper could figure out how everything went so wrong. It started when the clan started gathering in the kitchen after lunch. Shannon appeared from upstairs, wearing spic-and-span white instead of work clothes, and she peeled straight for the door the instant Matt showed up.

"Now, Dad. It's not that we don't want to help, but you don't need us. You're not wallpapering the whole kitchen, there's just one wall. Two more people would just get in your way." His daughter shot a meaningful look at Matt. "And we want you and Mrs. Neilson to have fun."

Coop had counted on the whole family having fun, as a way of underlining to Priss how well they all got on together. He capitulated, though. The kids hoped to go to a show, then a picnic at a friend's house, and Matt didn't get many Saturday afternoons off work.

More relevant, the two conspirators clearly thought it was a great idea for him and Priss to be alone. And he *did* want to be alone with her.

Just not quite under these circumstances.

The wallpapering project was supposed to be fun. He was *positive* it was going to be fun. Priss had picked out the pattern, not too feminine, a look of country with splashes of color against a cream background. All he wanted was to paper the one wall over the sink. There was a window in the middle of the wall. No big deal. He'd read the directions. You had to cut the stuff to fit, then dunk it in water, then put it up. No sweat.

The first strip went up like an angel. The second piece had to be cut. He cut it too short. By the time he snipped a replacement piece, the first strip was peeling down the wall. The stuff was as sticky as a shower in glue. He had to stand on the counter to put it up, which meant that he was hunched over like a dwarf and his head inevitably kept bumping the ceiling.

And Shortie, damn her, was suffering hiccups from laughing so hard.

"I'm not laughing *at* you, I'm laughing *with* you," she kept saying.

"And cats fly," he grumbled. "You think you could do better?"

"I know I could do better. I've had practice, you haven't. I keep telling you to sit down and pour yourself a glass of lemonade and just relax. I don't mind doing it. I love doing things like wallpapering."

Sit like a lazy dog while he watched her sweat and get the glueish junk all over her? *Not* likely. Besides, though he wasn't likely to admit it aloud, he loved making her laugh.

"The fair's next Saturday, right?" he asked her.

"Right. I'm stuck working most of the day—selling tickets in the morning, and manning a booth in the afternoon. Maybe you could take the kids?"

"I'd rather drive you. You'll be tired when it's over, and that way you'll have a ride. We can all start out together. If the kids want to leave at a different time, they can hoof it home. It's not that far a walk." He put up another strip and started squishing out the wrinkles. Priss was sitting cross-legged on the floor, cutting out the next piece. She claimed he wasn't allowed near the scissors again. While she had her hands full, he figured it was a good time to bring up a few things that he'd neglected to mention. "I've had several long talks with Shannon," he told her.

"Yeah?"

"Yeah. She's going to stay here, start school, live with me. Denise didn't like it, her being so far away, but we talked it out. She's getting along better here, it's as simple as that. I set some rules I thought were pretty strict, she's stuck by them. It's not a fast process, but she's gradually settling down, quieting down...." He hesitated, searching for the right words, then just said simply, "She's happier. I think, a lot, thanks to you, Shortie."

"All I ever did was talk with her a few times," Priss immediately denied. "You're the major influence on her, Coop. Not that you can save her from the trials of growing up, but it matters, that you listen to her, that you understand her temperament, that she knows she can count on you. You're her anchor. And I really think you made a good decision, having her stay with you."

Cooper raised his eyes to the ceiling. He should have known Priss would shift any credit for influencing Shannon on him. But his daughter wasn't the only subject on his mind, and he tried again. "I may have gotten a job offer," he mentioned casually.

She looked up. "I'll be darned. Don't tell me you went looking for employment?"

He cleared his throat. "I didn't want to. But someone in my life—a nagging, bossy woman, no one you'd know—put this bug in my ear about needing some kind of meaningful work. I don't want to name names. I'd probably never hear the end of it. And it's hard, real hard, for me to admit she was right."

"I'm going to forgive your calling me a bossy nag, Maitland, but only because I can't wait to hear more about this job offer."

He grinned. "Nothing's signed on the dotted line yet. So far it's just an offer. Had lunch with Redd Adkins from the bank and Jan Decker from the Chamber. Seems they want to see some new growth in our burg. New look, new life, something to bring new money into Bayville. They seem to think I could tackle a project like that."

Priss quit cutting, focusing all her attention on him. "I can't imagine where they got such an incredibly wild idea," she murmured.

He grinned again. "I may have mentioned to a few people that the local clinic is inadequate. That the health care industry is growing, that if we expanded in that area, and did it right, we could create jobs, widen the tax base and help ourselves without really changing the nature of the town. The next thing I knew, they were offering me the job."

"But you haven't taken it yet?"

"I'm still thinking about it. I know business, but I don't know diddly about the health care field. It'd be a lot to learn, a lot to put together." When he motioned, she handed him the next strip.

"It sounds like an impossible challenge. Your favorite kind."

Shortie knew him too well. He didn't try to deny it. And she'd known he needed serious work long before he was ready to admit it, so he didn't try to deny that, either. "There's no way that kind of job would fit in a controllable nine-to-five mold. There'd be night meetings. Some travel required."

"You're afraid it would get away from you? That you'd slip back into the pattern of working all the time again?" Priss asked quietly.

He hesitated before answering. "It happened before. And though my marriage to Denise always had some pitfalls, I know I was responsible for it really going downhill. It was like heroin—the push to achieve, then to achieve more. It consumed me. She needed time and attention, and I was never there. I didn't see that I was hurting her. I didn't see that she was lonely."

Priss cocked her head. "Are you going to take all the blame for that failed relationship or let her have a teensy bit? The last I knew, it took two to create problems."

"Neilson, I'm trying to tell you that I can be bullheaded and blind."

"I heard you," she said gently. "But it's easier for me to be cool about this, Maitland, because I have the nice advantage of some distance. Maybe I don't know your ex-wife, but if you let your whole life become work, I suspect there was something elementally wrong between the two of you. And you're not the same man now, Coop. You've grown. You've learned from your mistakes and you want different things. I think you'll probably have to juggle a while to find a natural balance, but I don't think you'll ever let work completely overtake the rest of your life again."

He looked at her. He didn't know how she did it, but every darn time they talked, her perspective and sensitivity put things in the right place. "I'm not sure I like it," he said dryly, "that you're smarter than I am, Shortie."

The corners of her mouth kicked up in an innocent, feminine grin. "I'm glad you believe that. Let's hope you keep that illusion for a long, long time. Ah . . . Coop? We have another strip coming loose."

Eventually the blasted wall was done. He cleaned up with his eyes on it, balefully waiting for the whole thing to come tumbling down, but it finally seemed to be sticking. There was a lot of leftover paper. Priss was cutting it up to line his drawers and cupboards. The drawers and cupboards already had paper, but she insisted that a new kitchen required fresh. She said it was a female ritual.

Cooper wasn't inclined to argue with anything as sacred as a female ritual. When his mess was cleaned up, he clunked ice cubes into two glasses and poured lemonade, watching her make a new disastrous mess with amusement. Pots and pans littered the floor, along with scissors and scraps of paper. She was fanny-up, her head stuck deep in a bottom cupboard, laying paper when she suddenly said, "Cooper?"

"Hmm?" He set a glass of lemonade down next to her.

"Something happened to me a long time ago. So long ago that maybe there's no point in mentioning it now. But you've always been so honest with me that I'm afraid it's going to nag on my conscience if I don't tell you."

Her tone was so conversational and casual that for a moment it didn't register that she was finally going to tell him what was wrong. Now. In her bare feet, with her head buried in that stupid cupboard, and her voice so breezy and light that it tore at his heart. All the oxygen seemed to be trapped in his lungs. He was afraid to move, afraid to breathe, for fear of doing or saying the wrong thing. "It's okay, whatever it is. Just tell me," he said.

"There was a boy once. He . . . assaulted me." As if that announcement were of no more importance than a weather forecast, she quickly moved on. "At the time, for a long time, I thought it was my fault. In fact, I suspect that eleven people on a twelve-person jury would say that I asked for exactly what I got. I willingly went out with him. I willingly got into a situation with him where we were alone. And I'll be the first to admit that I was naive and stupid. But I never asked for what happened. He knew what he was going to do. I didn't. In my worst nightmare, I never dreamed anything like that could happen—not to me."

Her head popped out of the cupboard. With her eyes averted from his, she rapidly unrolled another stretch of wallpaper. Go to her, cried his heart. Yet he sat absolutely still. Every masculine instinct warned him that she needed to tell this her own way or she wouldn't tell him at all. And right now, at least, she was still talking.

"I never told anyone. For one thing, I didn't think anyone would believe me. Why should anyone believe my word over his? For another, telling would have hurt the people closest to me, like my dad and my younger sisters—we all still had to live in this town. I had family to protect, Coop. And later, a husband and son."

"I understand."

"I'm hardly the only woman this has ever happened to. It's all over the media, that if this happens to you, you're supposed to talk and get counseling and help. But that isn't an automatic option for everyone. I think there are a lot of women who feel they have no choice but to keep silent. You do what you have to do. You make yourself forget it and you make yourself be strong and you go on."

Priss hadn't looked at him since she started talking. Now she did, a quick glance, a bare connection of soul-scared dark eyes meeting his. And still, her voice was even and light, a model of control. "Look, Coop. I knew telling you might change how you felt about me. And maybe you'd have never known, but I couldn't be positive about that. It seemed better to be honest now. But I understand . . . if you need to think about it. I know something like this sounds ugly. It *is* ugly—"

A sound came out of his throat that he couldn't stop. His whole body felt like a pit-hot volcano that had been building pressure for a thousand years.

It wasn't as if he hadn't known. All along he guessed that a man had hurt her. And he understood why she'd kept quiet. It was just like Priss, to believe she had to protect everyone else. It was just like her, to expect courage and strength from herself no matter what devastating blows life handed her. But she'd been afraid to tell him. Dread was in her eyes, as if she already anticipated that his feelings for her would automatically change. And the volcano blew.

He swooped down on her faster than a growly bear. The roll of paper thumped to the ground. Scraps

drifted out of her hands. He lifted her to her feet and
found her mouth, took her mouth, a kiss meant to seal
like a welder's brand. He never let up until both of
them were short of breath, and only then to roar at
her.

"You thought because that bastard did something
ugly, that I'd think something ugly about you? Maybe
you thought I'd be ashamed of you, see you suddenly
like soiled goods? Dammit, Priss. Maybe you even
thought I'd see his side?"

Her fingertips were on his face. Stroking. Touch-
ing. "I told you it wasn't cut-and-dried. He said it was
my fault. He said I'd asked for it. A lot of people
would believe him."

"I'm not a lot of people, Shortie. I'm the man who
loves you, and I thought you knew that."

"Coop, control yourself."

The hell he would. The hell he could. She didn't
weigh more than cotton fluff. Kissing her the whole
time, he carried her through the living room and down
the hall. His bedroom was in the back, and still in the
disaster stage of reconstruction. He'd torn out a wall,
added the deck and sliding glass doors. It still smelled
like sawdust and linseed oil. The doors were open, hot-
afternoon sun streaming on his rumpled king-size bed.
He hadn't made the bed. He never made beds. A shirt
was crumpled on a chair; a jumble of tools still clut-
tered a knotted-pine table. He'd never planned on
Priss seeing the room until it was finished and all
cleaned up. He'd never expected that there would be
any chance to make love with her, not this afternoon,
not here, not anywhere.

He thought, *My God, what's the matter with you?
You can't let this happen. Not like this. You'll risk
everything if you scare her.*

But her arms were wound like a lasso around his neck when he kicked the door closed. And her mouth, her soft fragile mouth, was glued beneath his with searing pressure.

She didn't seem scared. His weight was off balance when he tried to lay her down. He never meant to tumble on top of her. He'd have shifted, quickly, more aware than ever that Priss had reason to fear being pinned, especially under a man of his size. But when he tried to move, she hooked a slim slender leg around his thigh.

She didn't seem scared then, either.

He understood, in his head, that it was critically important for him to be gentle. Yet pictures kept flashing in his mind. Pictures of a small, infinitely fragile girl with laughing eyes and an unquenchable capacity for giving. So good. She'd always been so good, and he ached with a rage from deep inside him, thinking of the kind of guy who'd hurt her, thinking that he'd just like ten minutes alone with the jerk. He had to get rid of that rage. He never wanted Priss to associate him with force or anger, and her David, sure as hell, would never have expressed anger anywhere around her. He wasn't a saint like David. But he would try to be.

If Shortie, damn her, would give him a chance.

When he lifted up, buttons from his shirt popped all over the room. She'd yanked the material open rather violently.

"Sweetheart—"

She thumbed open the snap of his jeans, then pulled at that material, too. The zipper parted so fast that their future progeny would have been seriously jeopardized if he hadn't been wearing briefs.

"Um...sweetheart?"

She twisted up, pulled her T-shirt over her head, spun it around in a circle and then tossed it. For a flash of a second he caught her eyes. Liquid chocolate. Focused, melting hot, on him. He was getting the feeling that just possibly, just conceivably, a saint wasn't what she needed or wanted right now.

She pulled him down by the ears, opened her mouth against his mouth in a kiss of pure steam heat. A pillow flopped on the floor. She pushed the blanket and sheets free, then kissed him again, over and over, an orgy of kisses meant to tease and inflame. She angled a knee between his legs and rubbed against him, her spine arched so her belly and breasts rubbed against him, too.

He had another one of those feelings.

He couldn't just kick off his jeans because they wouldn't kick. The darn denim stuck to his legs. He fought free of them. Her shorts came off far easier, a scrap of white lace-trimmed panties with it.

When they were both bare, he tried to pull her on top of him, but Priss had other ideas. It wasn't as if the pixie could physically force him to do anything in this lifetime, but she *did* have a way of using a man's balance against him. She framed his face between her palms. "Your eyes are wet," she said fiercely. "That wasn't why I told you. To make you feel bad. Stop it, Coop. Stop thinking about it."

Priss seemed to be under the incredibly strange illusion that there were tears in his eyes. Hell. Maybe there were. But for the first time he comprehended how powerfully the past had a hold on her heart, because she was different now, in a way he could sense, see, feel. She was like a forest nymph, coming out of the dark shadows to embrace the sunlight. She didn't want him to feel bad. Evil didn't exist between them.

All touch was good. She wanted him to feel only good things and she kissed and stroked as if she could erase all memory of hurt with the sheer power of her feminine will. She moved her body like a love song, the music of yearning in her eyes, her touch a repeating chorus, her heart beating to a woman's rhythm of need. Her hands played the words that only he could hear, words just for him, and she'd have immersed him in that well of love forever if he'd let her.

When he swept her beneath him, her legs instinctively wrapped around his waist. He braced, anticipating her unconscious reaction of fear, but it never happened. There was no question what she wanted. She welcomed his weight, invited his complete possession. She took him in, drowning deep, with her eyes on his like a connection of souls. His mind spun, so submersed in her that nothing else existed. She was fire and softness, music and light, and temporarily, a less than patient lover. She needed him. Now. She wanted him with her, and she didn't want to wait.

She was good and strong and brave, but as vulnerable as precious treasure. He'd always known that she would be a dangerously demanding lover when she really let go. She belonged to him, with him, and he knew her body as he knew his own heartbeat. He deepened his thrusts until she tensed with the first spasm of pleasure, then another and another. He felt a shattering as his warmth and life spilled into her. She took him under, to a place of silk and moonshine, where ecstasy was her taste, her texture, and the only emotion he knew was loving her.

Afterward, he felt as whipped as if he'd climbed Mount Everest before lunch, but he couldn't stop looking at her. Her eyes were closed, her chest still heaving, her soft white skin like wet pearls. Wonder filled him, for his luck in finding this one unique and special woman, wonder for his luck in loving her. He leaned over and kissed the hollow between her breasts, tenderly, reverently, and then collapsed back on the pillow.

"Coop," she whispered, "I love you."

He thought he couldn't feel any more. He thought it wasn't possible to feel any more complete as a man. "I love you, too," he said fiercely, and made her smile. He started to pull up a sheet, but she tangled closer, cushioning her cheek against his shoulder. She wasn't cold.

"You took me out, Coop," she accused him sleepily.

"How many times do I have to tell you? It's the other way around." He stroked her hair. "I still remember the first day I saw you in the post office. I remember thinking that I was finally home and it was about time I changed my life around and quit looking for trouble. And there you were, with that short hair and that adorable fanny and those big eyes glaring at me, like don't-you-dare-try-messing-with-*me*-buster. A hundred pounds of trouble, but even then I knew it was too late. You were so sassy, Shortie. I'm afraid I was already in love."

"Well, I remember looking at those wrestler's shoulders and those sexy eyes and thinking that I was thankfully far too smart to mess with dynamite. In fact, I was convinced you were a serious health risk until that night in the rain when I threw you." She tilted her head. "I thought I'd killed you that night, Coop."

"You nearly did," he assured her.

"Hah. You were the one who knocked me for six. I couldn't stand the idea that I might have hurt you, that you willingly risked being hurt because of me. Even before that, you were like a sliver under my skin and about as hard to ignore as a mountain in my front yard."

"Obviously you're a woman who can move mountains, Priss."

In the sunlit bedroom, her eyes settled on him as if he was her only source of warmth and light. "You're the one who moved mountains," she said softly. "You were honest with me, in a way I never knew a man and a woman could be honest with each other. You made me feel things that I never thought I'd feel again. And the past . . . for the first time in my life, I know it's finally and completely buried." She hesitated, the smallest frown creasing her brow.

With the pad of his thumb, he smoothed out that frown. He'd never wanted to be the catalyst who made her remember the past, yet he was disturbingly aware that a wound that deep to the spirit carried inevitable scars. She was so proud, so stubbornly determined to believe that she'd never let it matter. Yet it had. From everything he knew of her, that incident had dominated her emotions, her choices, her whole life.

But no more, he thought. He would protect her, keep her safe. In a lifetime of nights, he would treasure her. In a lifetime of days, he could surely build up her feelings of security and healing confidence. He adored her. The way she'd made love—the way she was with him—infinitely reassured him that she felt the same way. For the first time he felt sure she was ready to talk about the future.

"Priss . . . I know we have things to talk out. I don't know if you want more children or where you want to live. I don't know how you want to tell the kids—or even how we'd handle the kids living in the same house. But those kinds of things we can work out. The bottom line is that you mean everything to me. I feel like I've been looking for you my whole life, and there's no way I could ever let you go. You're a part of my heart.''

Her palm, laying flat against his chest, went still. A shimmer of moisture glistened in her eyes. ''You're part of my heart, too,'' she whispered.

''Then marry me, Shortie.''

She knew the question was coming, and her lips even framed the ''yes'' he hoped to hear. Yet she didn't say it. She swallowed hard instead. He never thought he'd see fear in her eyes again—not with him—yet her gaze locked on his face with an echo of that old, old anxiety.

Cooper felt the raw taste of helplessness. Maybe, as a man, he was incapable of understanding all she'd had to emotionally deal with. But if there was a dragon she still had to face, he didn't know what it was. The sharp ache of pain thudded through his pulse. Her silence did not precisely mean a no.

But it was a world away from a yes.

And unless he understood what she was really afraid of, he knew, as sure as he breathed, that he was going to lose her.

Eleven

The annual Bayville summer fair was always held on the high school playing field. Clouds had threatened all day, but so far the rain had held off. Priss had loved the fair for as long as she could remember. The noise was incessant and the atmosphere rowdy. At one end, there were rented rides—a ferris wheel and carousel. At the other end, hogs were roasting in barrels, along with fresh corn on the cob dripping with butter. Dozens of booths lined the spaces in between. The games were set up so that every child won something. The baking contests never lacked for volunteer judges. Mr. Stevens traditionally did his juggling act. Babe O'Connell jammed on a wig and played a hurdy-gurdy. The local English teacher did magic tricks. By midafternoon, as it should be, there wasn't a kid running around who wasn't filthy.

And temporarily, Priss thought dismally, they were all lined up in front of the cardboard sign that read Dunk A Teacher. She'd volunteered to participate because, tarnation, no one else ever did. And the booth helped pay for school band uniforms—a great cause. It was just that she forgot, every year, how many kids in this town really knew her.

"Is that you, Jimmy Simpson? Before you aim that ball, you'd better remember that I'm going to have you for biology come September. Think detentions. Think failing grades. Think how miserable I can make your life—"

He wasn't impressed with her threats. None of them were. The red ball zoomed unerringly for the white plank board behind her head, hit it with a thwack and down she went with a splash one more time.

She came up sputtering and gasping—hamming it up was required behavior for the dunkee. So was wearing an orange-and-white polka-dotted clown suit, which Priss didn't mind as she would have felt uncomfortable parading in a wet bathing suit in public. She faked huge shivers because they pleased the crowd, but truthfully the water in the huge barrel was as tepid as bathwater. She wasn't cold; she wasn't uncomfortable. She frankly loved pleasing the kids, and there wasn't a way on this earth that she wouldn't be having a great time . . . if there wasn't an aching hole in her heart as big as the sky.

Cooper had driven her and the kids to the fair. She'd seen Shannon, she'd seen Matt, but for more than an hour now she hadn't seen *him*. The devil had revved up the crowd by throwing the first ball that dunked her. He'd had fun, but his eyes . . . the way he looked at her wasn't the same since he asked her to marry him. She hadn't said no, only asked him to wait, but she knew she'd hurt him. It weighed on her heart like a sack of nails. All week, he'd had little to say. She hadn't once heard him laugh. His face had drawn lines, was the wrong color, and he was quiet, subdued.

Priss needed to give him an answer—and an explanation. Yet neither was simple. Telling him about the assault had been painful, but Coop had overwhelmingly proven how he felt about her. When he'd asked her to marry him, her heart had all but spilled out a yes. Then, suddenly, she'd panicked. A fistful of anxiety had jammed in her throat.

She thought she'd never have that old sick feeling of being pulled down into quicksand again. When she was seventeen, she'd nearly drowned in feelings of guilt and shame. She'd believed she wasn't a good person anymore, that she'd never be a good person again. That had nothing to do with Coop—it had to do with that jerk—yet suddenly she'd been paralyzingly scared that she'd never be able to make a marriage work. She would disappoint him. She'd felt inadequate, not good enough, not...equal.

A redheaded boy with a nose full of freckles stepped in front of her. Priss forced a smile on her face, forced herself to laugh and joke. The tears of a clown, she thought with weary humor. *But you can't be thinking about Cooper now, Neilson. And you, if anyone, should know how to hide your feelings.*

It was more than an hour later before some kind soul blew a shrill whistle. Her stint at the booth was finally over. Amid exuberant boos and protests from a line of kids still dying to dunk her, she climbed down from the platform, grabbed her knapsack and headed straight for the women's rest room.

After peeling off the soaking clown suit, she rubbed down with a towel, then tugged on white jeans and an Irish green top and sandals. No brush, no bra, no lipgloss. She'd forgotten all three. *Typical, Priss.* With her sunburned cheeks and spiky mop of hair, she looked younger than the kids, but there was no help for it.

Heading back outside, she quickly stashed the clown suit and knapsack in the supply tent, then aimed for the camper selling drinks and snacks. Her voice was hoarse, her throat desert-dry. She wanted badly to find Cooper but it shouldn't take more than seconds to pick up something tall and blessedly cool with ice.

She took two steps, rummaged in her purse for a dollar, then abruptly changed her mind. A few feet away, standing in line, Bric was buying cotton candy for his young ones.

Priss spun around.

Whenever she had to face him in town, she did. But there was another place to get a drink at the far end of the grounds, so facing him wasn't necessary. If Bric even remembered what he'd done, he never showed it. If he felt any guilt, he never showed that, either. Yet not once, in all these years of acting "normal" around him, had she ever failed to feel a sick burr in her stomach when she was near him.

"Priss?"

Cooper. She heard his voice even before she spotted him in the crowd. He was only a few feet away, leaning against a picnic table. As if her sandals had wings, she sprinted toward him. He extended a tall foam cup. "Iced tea," he said. "I thought you might be thirsty."

"Heavens, I am. Thanks." On the spot, she chugged a long gulp. The ice chinked against her teeth and the liquid soothed her throat.

"The kids gave you quite a workout."

"Every year I tell myself I'll never do that booth again, but every year... I don't know. The kids love it so much." She smiled at him, when what she desperately wanted to do was walk into those long strong arms and be held. A week ago, it would have been natural, even automatic, to swing an arm around his waist and lift her face. He'd have welcomed the chance to kiss her then. He'd have let her hug him forever if she asked. Now, she wasn't sure.

"Priss?"

"Hmm?" The sun shot gold in his brown hair. He was dressed in a short-sleeved shirt and jeans, nothing unusual, yet her eyes hungered for the look of him. He was so much man. There was so much character in his strong square features, so much vital energy, such an endless, huge capacity for love. Had she ever had the choice *not* to fall in love with him?

"What would you like me to do with him, honey? You want him shot, beaten, ridden out of town on a rail?"

"Pardon?" Priss blinked, assuming that she'd misheard him. His question seemed to come from nowhere.

Coop jerked his head in the direction of the tall blond man handing cotton candy to two children. "I'm talking about Eastman. And I'm asking you what you want me to do about him."

Her palms were suddenly slippery. She dropped the cup on the picnic table before it had a chance to slip from her hands. She'd told Coop about her attacker, but she'd never named the man. She knew she hadn't.

"I did a lot of thinking this past week. About you and me—and about him." Cooper's gaze honed on her face. "He's between us. He's between you and everything else in your life. I understand why you never pressed charges, why you never told. In your shoes, I'd have done the same thing. But that secret has preyed on your mind like a brickload of guilt, hasn't it, Shortie? You could never shake it. Even for a second. It's on your mind every day of your life."

"I'm not sure what you mean."

"All these years, you've had to worry that he would do it to someone else." His gaze was as relentless as the hot beating sun. "I should have realized it before. God knows, I know you. You'd save a kitten at the risk of your own neck. Your whole nature is to protect. And you protected certain people by keeping quiet, but there was the catch-22. By *not* talking, there were people you couldn't protect. Like his wife. I've watched you a couple of times with Janet. You talk to her, you look at her, like a doctor examining a patient. You would have felt responsible if he hurt her, wouldn't you?"

"Yes." Again, her throat felt parched dry. "I made a friend of her, tried to watch over her—"

"And it wasn't just her. Your dad told me that you lead a women's group at the church."

"Yes," she admitted again. She suddenly felt cold all over, aching cold and alone. A dozen people ambled by. She knew every name, every face. Why was Cooper making her talk about this *now?*

"And that was the reason you chose to teach, wasn't it? Biology is a requirement—every teenage girl in town takes your class. You could watch over all of them. You could keep a special look out for a particularly vulnerable girl. A girl like Shannon, for instance.''

She lifted her head.

"I think my daughter is a lot like you were once, Shortie. You were never so wild and you don't have a selfish bone in your body. But you showed all your emotions on the surface. You were naive about life and you never thought anyone would hurt you. Like Shannon. She's the type, isn't she, who would be easy prey for a bastard like Bric?" He said quietly, "Priss . . . I want you to confront him."

She felt as stunned and hurt as if he'd hit her. She couldn't believe he would suggest such a thing. She'd been so sure that Coop loved her, that of any man on earth, he would protect her. Never that he'd throw her to the wolf.

His tone was curt and low. People milled all around them. He never broke contact with her eyes. "He isn't paying the price for what he did. You are. Are you going to let him do that to you forever? You've spent almost twenty years trying to protect everyone else, believing you'd be responsible if he did it again. The only one who can stop it is you, Priss. Do it. Confront him."

"You don't know what you're asking of me," she said fiercely.

"Yeah," he said, "I do." He straightened, and without another glance at her, walked away.

She couldn't, she told herself. She couldn't possibly confront Bric. Even considering the idea made her violently nauseous. Coop was a dog. An inhuman, insensitive, unfeeling low-down cur to expect her to do such a thing. Damned how she ever thought she loved him.

Damned why her heart splintered in a million jagged pieces when she watched him walk away. She couldn't breathe. She hurt too much to even cry. She pushed away from the picnic table, feeling sickheaded, the blood slamming in her pulse. It didn't matter where she went, as long as it was away from there.

Or so she believed. An echo of laughter drifted through the crowd. A dozen yards away, Bric was sitting at a long table with his wife. Their kids had scattered. Priss recognized most of the other adults at the table—men, primarily, all involved in a boisterous discussion of local politics. Bric's blond head towered over the others. He was wearing a red shirt and tennis shorts and he'd nicked himself shaving on his right cheek.

Priss never anticipated being close enough to him to notice such a personal thing as a shaving nick...until she found herself there, standing at the edge of the table, exchanging greetings with Janet until Bric turned his head. When he glanced at her, her stomach twisted with acid. "Well, hi there, honey. Heard you really brought in the bucks with your booth."

"I hope so," she said crisply. "Is there any chance I could talk to you for a minute?"

"Why, sure." He motioned her to a spare seat.

She shook her head and glanced at Janet. "I just need to ask him something away from the noise. I promise to have him back in five minutes. Would that be okay?"

"No problem," Janet responded curiously.

Bric waggled his eyebrows and rose with a charming smile. "I'd never refuse a beautiful woman who wants to be alone with me."

"This won't take long," she repeated to Janet.

There was no place to beg, borrow or steal any privacy at the fair. At least temporarily, though, there was no one behind the canvas supply tent. "Is this good enough?" he asked her, obviously still humored by the suggestion that she wanted to see him alone.

It never occurred to him, she thought, never, that she'd ever have the guts to do anything. She'd been helpless. He always knew it. She'd never talk. He'd known that, too.

It hurt like a raw wound, that Cooper had to light into her before she could see it.

"Well? What can I do for you, darlin'?"

"Nothing. Ever. There's just something I want to say. Something I should have said to you a long time ago." She never stopped for a breath. "As far as I know, you never hurt anyone else. But just so you know, I would never have kept quiet if I thought you had, no matter what the consequences might have been for me. And if I ever hear that you've gone after another woman in this town, I'll expose you for the slime you are."

"What?" His charming smile froze in place.

"You heard me."

"God, do you hold a grudge. You're talking about all those years ago, aren't you? As I remember it, honey, you liked it a little rough—"

She didn't know she was going to do it. She'd taken self-defense to be able to protect herself, but it went against every grain, every principle and moral she had, to physically hurt anyone else. Yet her fist shot up, like a miniature jet-propelled rocket, and smashed with enormous satisfaction into his arrogant nose.

It wiped his smile off just fine.

She didn't have anything else to say to him. She whipped around and walked away. It was only when she turned the corner of the tent that she realized her hand was broken. It had to be. It stung in about fifty million places. Tears spattered from her eyes like acid. It was all Cooper's fault. As soon as she caught up with Coop, he was going to pay some serious repercussions for making her go through this.

But first she had to find him.

She desperately wanted to find him.

A dark cluster of clouds streaked over the late-afternoon sun. The hot day suddenly turned cool. A gusty wind stole a child's balloon. Women, laughing, chased after runaway napkins and hustled to cover plates of food. Priss saw everyone she knew—everyone but Coop.

She found her son shooting ducks, trying to win a stuffed animal for Shannon. She told them she wanted to go home. They could either walk home later or come with her. They wanted to stay until the fireworks, assuming the rain held off, and that was okay with Priss. But did they know where Cooper was? Had they seen him?

They hadn't. The only place left to look was the square of side street where he'd parked the car. The Lincoln hadn't been moved. If Priss had to get home, she knew he taped a spare key in the gas tank. She fiercely wanted to be home. But not without him. Never, she thought, without him again.

She leaned against the fender and waited. Minutes ticked by. Not many. Her eyes were peeled on the ticket entrance to the fair, so she saw him the instant he strode through the gate. His hair was all disheveled in the wind, but it wasn't until he came closer that she noticed the button torn off his shirt, the ragged tear in the shoulder.

There was so much she wanted to say to him but not at that instant. Not if he was hurt. She rushed toward him. "Cooper! What happened to you?"

"Nothing that matters. I was clumsy, ran into a fence post. Let's see your hand."

She frowned, trying to see beneath his shirt's tear for damages. He seemed okay. She saw the beginning swell of a small bruise, but no broken skin. "Where on earth did you run into a fence?" She suddenly lifted her head. "How'd you know about my hand?"

He neither answered her nor seemed to even remember his own injuries. As fast as he reached her, he swiftly claimed her wrist and turned her palm over. He swore when he saw her red-raw knuckles. "Let's get you home and get some ice on that."

He had her home faster than two shakes of a lamb's tail. The minute they were inside her kitchen, he held her wrist under cool running tap water and fumbled through her cupboards for a plastic bag to hold ice. "Nothing's broken or you wouldn't be able to flex it. But I'm afraid those knuckles are going to swell if we don't get some ice on them. And where's your aspirin?"

She didn't give a holy patootie where her aspirin was. "You saw me talking to Bric, didn't you? That's how you knew about my hand."

Cooper avoided her eyes. "Whether you believe it or not, it was the hardest thing I ever did, letting you go near him alone. But you did it, Shortie. You fought your dragon and you won. With no help from me or anyone else."

"Possibly that was something I needed to know I could do alone," she agreed slowly. "But I think you were in the wings in case anything went wrong. And I think you must have had a word or two with him after I left. That's why I couldn't find you. That's why your shirt is all torn up. You didn't run into any fence. You went after Bric.''

"Nonsense," Cooper said flatly.

"Maitland, would you quit dithering with that darned ice and look at me?''

He did. Her heart swelled like a love-stuffed balloon. He looked at her the old way, the wicked way. As if he liked the look of her engine. As if she was a country he might not mind taking over. As if she was his whole world.

But he didn't move toward her. He didn't move at all. The man she loved understood her infinitely well. She expected strength of herself. She couldn't come to a lover as less than an equal, and Priss suspected that he would never outright admit that he had been there to protect her against Eastman.

Eastman didn't matter. Not anymore. The man with the bleak, lonesome blue eyes who was so unsure of her feelings was all that mattered to her. "You were right," she said softly. "I should have confronted him before. I tried so hard to put it behind me, forget it ever happened. But it was always there. I would have hurt other people by telling. But by keeping the secret, I was always afraid he was going to do it to someone else. That guilt . . . I could never shake it. It infected my whole life.''

"I know, love.''

"Maybe threatening him with exposure will make a difference. I don't know. You can't put a conscience in a horse's behind. All I really know is that confronting him changed how I feel about *me,* Coop. For the first time in so many years, I didn't feel like a victim anymore." She took a long, painful breath. "I loved David. I was the best wife for him that I knew how to be. In my heart I believe, I need to believe, that I made him happy."

"There's no doubt in my mind, sweetheart," he said.

"But I love you more, Cooper. I love you in such a deeper, different way. It was like that victim mind-set stopped me from reaching out to all I could be, all I wanted to be, as a woman. You made me see that I was settling for less. That was all I thought I could have."

Even in the dimly lit kitchen, she could see the liquid sheen in his eyes. She'd seen Coop cry twice for her now. She never wanted to see it again. She sprang for him, her arms extended. He swallowed her up in a monster-size hug, his lips in her hair, his eyes squeezed closed.

"I thought I'd lost you," he said fiercely.

"I thought I'd lost *you*. When you walked away from me, I thought I was going to die. It took me forever to figure out that was a risk you were taking for me out of love. You've taken a lot of risks for me, Maitland. I've never imagined a man could cause me so much trouble. You're like trying to deal with a lit keg of dynamite. Everything with you is all or nothing. And now I'm afraid you're stuck paying the price—because you showed me that I could have it all. With you." On tiptoe, she pelted kisses on his cheeks, his nose, his lips. "I want a ring."

"You sound sure, Shortie."

"I am *very* sure."

"You don't think this is rather sudden?"

Unfortunately when Coop was truly happy, he had a nasty tendency to tease. She ignored that sassy question, and showered his face with more kisses. "I want to be married in my father's church. And after all the reconstruction work you've done, I suppose we'd better live in your house. We'll move upstairs, on the same floor as Shannon. Matt can take the downstairs bedroom. And we need to tell the kids. Soon. Like today. We'll do that together.''

"All these sudden demands," he mused.

"It's your own fault. Only a strong woman could handle you, Coop. I'm afraid you're going to be stuck with a terribly demanding wife."

"I think I can bear up."

"I think you can, too." She framed his face with her hands. "I love you, Cooper Maitland. With all my heart. You have no idea how happy I'm going to make you. You have no idea how happy you're going to make *me*."

But he already had the idea. He'd had it from the moment he laid eyes on her. Priss was strong and she was good and she was—and always would be—the love of his heart. What she'd been through mattered. But the life they would build together mattered more. The right kind of love, he'd discovered with her, really could move mountains.

And it was more than a mountain of love he felt for Priss.

*   *   *   *   *

**Relive the romance...
Harlequin and Silhouette
are proud to present**

by Request

A program of collections of three complete novels by the most requested authors with the most requested themes. Be sure to look for one volume each month with three complete novels by top name authors.

In June: **NINE MONTHS** Penny Jordan
Stella Cameron
Janice Kaiser

Three women pregnant and alone. But a lot can happen in nine months!

In July: **DADDY'S HOME** Kristin James
Naomi Horton
Mary Lynn Baxter

Daddy's Home... and his presence is long overdue!

In August: **FORGOTTEN PAST** Barbara Kaye
Pamela Browning
Nancy Martin

Do you dare to create a future if you've forgotten the past?

Available at your favorite retail outlet.

HARLEQUIN Silhouette

REQ-G

SILHOUETTE® Desire®

HAWK'S WAY

HAWK'S WAY—where the Whitelaws of Texas run free till passion brands their hearts. A hot new series from Joan Johnston!

Look for the first of a long line of Texan adventures, beginning in April with THE RANCHER AND THE RUNAWAY BRIDE (D #779), as Tate Whitelaw battles her bossy brothers—and a sexy rancher.

Next, in May, Faron Whitelaw meets his match in THE COWBOY AND THE PRINCESS (D #785).

Finally, in June, Garth Whitelaw shows you just how hot the summer can get in THE WRANGLER AND THE RICH GIRL (D #791).

Join the Whitelaws as they saunter about HAWK'S WAY looking for their perfect mates . . . only from Silhouette Desire!

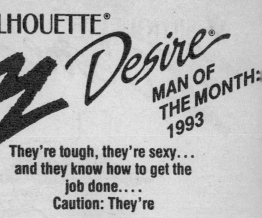

SILHOUETTE® Desire®

MAN OF THE MONTH: 1993

**They're tough, they're sexy...
and they know how to get the
job done....
Caution: They're**

MEN AT WORK

Blue collar...white collar...these men are working overtime
to earn your love.

January:	Businessman Lyon Cantrell in Joan Hohl's LYON'S CUB
February:	Landscaper-turned-child-saver David Coronado in Raye Morgan's THE BACHELOR
March:	Woodworker Will Lang in Jackie Merritt's TENNESSEE WALTZ
April:	Contractor Jake Hatcher in Dixie Browning's HAZARDS OF THE HEART (her 50th Silhouette Book)
May:	Workaholic Cooper Maitland in Jennifer Greene's QUICKSAND
June:	Wheeler-dealer Tyler Tremaine in Barbara Boswell's TRIPLE TREAT

And that's just your first six months' pay! Let these men make
a direct deposit into your heart. MEN AT WORK...only from
Silhouette Desire!

MOM93JJ